Virtual SeXUaL Reality

RED FOX DEFINITIONS

CHLOË RAYBAN

Virtual SeXual Reality

RED FOX DEFiniTiONS

A Red Fox Book
Published by Random House Children's Books
20 Vauxhall Bridge Road, London SW1V 2SA

A division of The Random House Group Limited
London Melbourne Sydney Auckland
Johannesburg and agencies throughout the world

First published in Great Britain by The Bodley Head 1994

This edition published by Red Fox 2001

1 3 5 7 9 10 8 6 4 2

Printed and bound in Great Britain by Clays Ltd, St Ives PLC

The Random House Group Limited Reg. No. 9540009

www.randomhouse.co.uk

ISBN 0 09 941752 9

The Random House Group Limited supports The Forest Stewardship
Council (FSC®), the leading international forest certification organisation.
Our books carrying the FSC label are printed on FSC® certified paper.
FSC is the only forest certification scheme endorsed by the leading
environmental organisations, including Greenpeace. Our
paper procurement policy can be found at
www.randomhouse.co.uk/environment

One

Absolutely none of this would have happened if it hadn't been for Chuck. Not that you could say it was his fault or anything.

Chuck had called me up on Friday night and after a lot of beating about the bush had said, 'What are you doing tomorrow, anyway?'

(Always a question that demands answering technique – say you've got something on and you've talked yourself out of the not-to-be-missed-event-of-the-century – admit the diary page is blank, and you've landed yourself with an overdose of Charles Nevil Davis.)

'Not sure yet. Why?'

'Just wondered.'

'I need some new cowboy boots – might go shopping with Franz.'

'Oh really?' (Barely disguised interest.)

Francesca, otherwise known as Franz is Fifth Form's Class Tart – it's OK, she wouldn't mind me saying so – I mean, she's got the lot – a body that goes in and out in all the approved places, the prescribed leg length, she can pout like Vanessa Paradis without looking obvious – boys simply go ape-s*** over her – and, maddeningly enough, she's actually nice with it.

'What were you thinking of doing?' I asked.

'There's this brilliant VR Exhibition on at Olympia.'

'What's VR? Sounds like some disease.'

'Virtual Reality, ignorant-child. You know, computer-generated experience – wicked – you ought to come along.'

'I think I'll give it a miss, thanks.'

I'd suffered this sort of thing in the past. Once a male gets a whiff of hi-tech in his nostrils, there's no holding him. He starts treating you like some type of life form that's been by-passed by evolution. If he condescends to explain anything, it's communicated ve-ry slow-ly and very patiently in nursery language.

'Then I guess I'll have to make do with Alex's company.'

Dropping this little gem of information, Chuck was about to ring off.

'If we get through shopping early enough, we might join you,' I cut in, in as laid back a way as I could manage.

'OK. We should be there three-thirtyish – we'll hang around outside for a bit if you like, in case you turn up.'

'Might see you there, then,' I said and hung up.

Boy!

I was on the phone right away to Franz.

'What are you doing tomorrow afternoon?'

'No idea.'

'How do you fancy going to an exhibition at Olympia?'

'Not a lot. Why?'

'Chuck and Alex are going.'

'*Definitely not* in that case.'

'Why's that?'

'Alex is a prat.'

Before I had a chance to ask in what specific form his prattishness had manifested itself, Franz had deftly moved the conversation on to another tack. She rang off before I found a suitable moment to enquire further.

Next day, I was standing outside Olympia at three-twenty-seven in the new cowboy boots – which I'd bought in a bit of a hurry actually, in order to get there on time. Applying a third coat of lip gloss, I was standing directly under the 'V' of a vast sign which read:

VIRTUAL REALITY
– Everything you never dreamed of –

So I simply couldn't be missed.

As a sea of blue jeans swept by, I waited with nothing better to do than ponder on that mystery of the universe – how from a single indigo dye, nature could produce such infinite variety . . .

Then a familiar pair of 501s detached itself from the general flow.

'Hi there,' said Chuck.

'Hi . . .' I said, observing in one lightning glance that he was being closely followed by . . . no one.

'Where's Alex?'

'Oh he couldn't make it,' said Chuck with forced casualness.

This didn't fool me. Basically, I realized I had been lured under false pretences. You see, I was getting wise to the decoy system. It works like this – guys like Chuck, who are pretty low on sexual charisma, use guys like Alex (who is by universal reckoning as horny as hell) as decoys. If the whole thing is played right, the decoy can attract enough of the opposite sex around them to make the low-charisma guy seem quite a catch. (And if you're thinking that's why I hang around with Franz, you can stop right now – she's my best friend for godsake.)

Then it suddenly occurred to me that it was most probable that Chuck hadn't actually told Alex that Franz was coming. In fact . . . it now seemed highly likely that he hadn't even invited Alex – he'd just been using the promise of a glimpse of him as bait.

'Where's Franz?' asked Chuck.

'She wouldn't come. She said something about Alex being a prat.'

'Really?' said Chuck, the little lines around his mouth displaying just the faintest suggestion of smugness.

'What's up with those two?'

Chuck shrugged. 'I wouldn't know.'

Something told me that Chuck was concealing a load of gossip that wasn't destined for female ears.

'Go on, tell.'

'No, honestly – no idea. Come on, let's get inside. You have got some cash on you?'

I followed Chuck to the pay desk and parted with seven pounds. Seven pounds! And this wasn't even an exhibition I wanted to see, for godsake!

Once inside, Chuck set off at one hell of a pace leaving me to trail along behind. He didn't even bother to look over his shoulder to see if I was following. Maybe 'the pleasure of my company' had not been the major incentive for the invitation. Or maybe he was just playing it cool . . .

In fact, one way and another, as the afternoon progressed it was turning out to be something of a disaster. I'd invested seven lousy pounds in the hope of nurturing a flicker of interest from Alex and I hadn't even had a sighting.

The exhibition itself was enough to bring on serious stress-related symptoms. It was full of dizzying computer-animated screens battling for attention. On all sides 'state-of-the-art hardware' blinked and beeped and burped at us – or droned out loop-taped messages in that kind of adenoidal voice that aliens have in Dr Who. Harassed Dads on weekend duty and small boys in shell suits were queuing expectantly for entrance to a variety of hi-tech booths. These were the actual Virtual Reality *experiences*. Surrounding them were loads of stands where hangers-on were selling computer back-ups and bolt-ons and touting a mind-boggling variety of 'user-friendly' software.

Chuck, of course, was in his element. He had already armed himself with a plastic carrier which was rapidly being filled with hi-tech unfathomabilia doled out to him by a load of Miss Essex rejects in leotards and monogrammed sashes.

Eventually, Chuck came to a halt beside a ramp with a shorter queue than some, which bore the slogan, 'Ruler of the Universe – experience the thrills of space racing – £6.00 for two persons'.

'How about it?' he said.

'Six quid – you must be joking.' I was down to my last fiver and could frankly have killed for a coffee.

'Tell you what, I'll pay for both of us and that'll cover the three quid I owe you from the flicks last week.'

'But I don't even want to go on the wretched thing.'

But we'd joined the queue anyway and we waited, bickering quite amicably, until our turn came.

Once inside, we had to put on odd kind of dusting gloves and head gear like crash helmets. Then we were strapped to our seats which frankly freaked me out because I knew I was highly likely to want to make a quick getaway.

After waiting what seemed like an age in total darkness which was so-oo freaky – it was just like it must feel to be dead, if not worse – quite suddenly the whole 'experience' leapt into life.

Painful as it is to relive the whole thing, I'll try to describe it for you:

Filling my field of vision was a kind of three-dimensional see-through cockpit. I was 'in' what seemed to be a space shuttle designed by someone with a certifiable disregard for

5

passenger safety – the view below was of Earth – I could just make out the boot bit of Italy and the Mediterranean, which looked much the same colour as it does from the beach at Cap d'Antibes, which was pretty surprising considering that, give or take the odd thousand, it was roughly three million miles away. When I summoned the nerve to turn my head, I could see another spaceship. I guessed this was meant to be Chuck's. Then a voice in my ear said, 'Prepare to commence racing, grasp your RGS – maximum ignition will occur at the end of countdown.'

My stomach sank in time with the count 5 . . . 4 . . . 3 . . . 2 . . . 1 . . . zero!

Suddenly, a vast force seemed to be squeezing me through the back of my seat. And everything outside started shooting past in a fuzzy blur. I closed my eyes and hung on for dear life.

I just kept praying I wouldn't be sick in my space helmet and wondering whether, if I was, I would get electrocuted. And even worse how this would just confirm in Chuck's eyes how amazingly wimpish girls are.

Basically, the sensation was like being sucked backwards, at approximately the speed of light, through an immensely large and powerful vacuum cleaner, while in the meantime the whole universe was being forced in the opposite direction so fast it was being stretched out of shape like the stripes in toothpaste. I sat there with my fists clenched in the gloves praying for it all to be over.

It went on forever!

Well, almost.

At last the screaming in my ears died down and faded away with some electronic bleeping noises. My hands were released from the gloves and I managed to undo the seat belt. The helmet was lifted off and I staggered out.

I met Chuck on the ramp.

'Wicked!' he said. 'Wasn't that mental!?'

I was too shattered to disagree, so I nodded weakly.

'That bit when we went through the asteroid belt – boy the way those things came at you, sparks were flying off your ship but you just kept going. Some nerve!'

Since I had had my eyes closed at the time, I accepted the praise with due modesty.

'How's about I treat you to another go to see if I can get even?' said Chuck.

'Actually, I'm a bit bored with that one,' I managed to say.

'Really! Well, in that case let's take a tour around and choose what to go on next,' he suggested.

I looked at the size of the place and wondered how far round I could get before I was talked into another 'experience'.

'Actually I could really do with a coffee,' I said. 'And then I ought to be making tracks.'

'But we've only just arrived!' said Chuck. Then he caught sight of my face. 'You feeling all right?'

'Yes, fine, why?' I lied.

'Not suffering from – you know – girls' troubles, PMT or something,' he asked with that exasperating mixture of male concern and condescension.

'No, I am not,' I replied, huffily.

'Sorry, just thought you looked a bit off, that's all.'

'Thanks a lot.'

'Well, if you're sure you're all right. You have your coffee and I'll look around. Let's say we meet up by the main exit in an hour or so. But it seems like a hell of a waste of seven pounds to me.'

'Huh,' I thought, as I watched Chuck stride off into the crowd swinging his carrier. 'Men!'

I queued up alone for my coffee at a bar on a little carpeted bit cordoned off by ropes on poles. Propped up at a plastic leaning post, drinking hot brownish liquid and wondering

7

what creature non-dairy creamer came from, I was trying very hard to forget I had feet.

The afternoon had been an unequivocal disaster. I wondered gloomily what Alex was actually doing. Which naturally led on to wondering why, precisely, Franz had called him a prat and how she had actually managed to get their relationship to a stage intimate enough to make such a discovery.

Males are a constant mystery. It's pretty freaky actually. I mean, to think that somewhere out of the mass of seething masculinity there is one of them actually destined – with the same kind of inevitability as A-levels and old age – for me . . .

Then again it's even more freaky to think maybe there isn't . . .

Imagine having to spend the rest of one's sexually active life trawling singles clubs full of fun-loving under-30s. Or worse, being reduced to placing advertisements in the back of the local paper – '*Lively, long-legged female from good family, non-smoker* [it's now three whole days since I last gave up] *seeks divine sun-bronzed hunk (17+) for desperately passionate, long-lasting relationship*'.

My sister Jemima, who's twenty-so-retired-from-the-scene says not to worry – there's someone for everyone. It's just a matter of lowering your standards until you find them.

So much for the cynicism of age. (In actual fact, she's out of the running anyway because she's married, poor dear – all a ghastly mistake and partly my fault – but that's a long story.)

My mother isn't quite so disillusioning. She comes out with quaint but comforting things like 'Your Mr Right will come along', and then ruins them by adding 'Look how I met your father.'

Actually, I have to admit that so far I haven't been wildly successful at trapping the ideal mate. It's a subject of some considerable concern as a matter of fact, as I'm rapidly heading for that landfall age of sixteen. Franz once remarked that if nothing had happened to you by the age of sixteen, it probably never would. Naturally I had agreed; we were both about twelve at the time so this far distant threat hadn't really got to me but now it was positively looming.

As I reached the dregs at the bottom of my 'coffee', I stared into the crowds and considered various candidates as they passed. (Guys do the same thing with girls, you know. You can even catch them at it sometimes – in buses and tubes and things.)

I was just sizing up Mr Umpteen when I got this odd kind of sensation. It was as if the whole of humanity had been kind of dropped into a vast universal episode of *Blind Date* with the choice of male restricted to those with peculiar trousers and a particularly humourless line in wit. I almost expected, at any minute, that some extra-terrestrial voice would say – 'Cum on Joustine, it's your turn to choose but don't choose until our Graham has had time to recap . . .'

As I came to the end of this gloom-inducing stream of consciousness, I found I had finished my dregs and felt out of pure altruism I ought to release my leaning post to the lengthening queue.

I wandered along still deeply musing about love, luck, lust and the lack of any of these in my life, so I hardly noticed that I was making my way round the outer perimeter of the exhibition. This was a kind of no-man's land where stalls were displaying a load of tacky giftware – things like non-slip writing pads and pens with blondes whose clothes disappeared when you turned them upside down, and hologram badges of supporting-role Disney characters.

Then I realized I was lost. I was standing in one corner of the building under a sign which said 'WEST'. Olympia is a very large stadium and my feet by now were truly killing me. Since I had no idea at which point of the compass the main exit was situated, this sign was particularly unhelpful and inappropriate. I had also just reached the depressing conclusion that it would most definitely have been wiser to have bought the larger size of cowboy boots and I was wondering whether a coat of clear nail varnish over the soles would render these returnable . . . when a voice in my ear said: 'Hello, my name's Julie. Can I interest you in a free demonstration?'

I had barely taken note of the fact that I had landed up in front of this really weird booth.

It had no neon sign, no flashing lights or bleeping noises. It just had an ordinary notice in slightly crooked stuck-on letters, which read:

ALTERNATIVE REALITY
Create a totally new image for yourself
FREE DEMONSTRATION

I hesitated – which, in retrospect, I realize was a mistake.

'I can see you're interested,' continued the voice.

'Julie', I assessed with one lightning glance, was the type of woman who didn't take kindly to a refusal. She was a small person heavily into costume jewellery. Partially obscured by the weight of giltware, she was wearing a purple Courtelle two-piece which led down to those truly dire tights with little bits of diamanté encrusted on them. To complete the effect with a memorably bizarre touch, she had on a pair of gleaming scarlet patent leather stilettos.

'Oh well, no, I don't think . . .' I started.

'It will only take a minute,' she said briskly.

I glanced at my watch. I still had time to kill before I was due to meet Chuck.

She whisked aside a curtain and revealed the interior of what looked remarkably like a railway-station photo booth. Inside, there was the usual seat facing a mirror.

A seat! (My toes were feeling as if they'd been through a rubbish compactor.)

'Oh well, if it really doesn't take long . . .' I said and sank thankfully on to it.

The curtain was pulled across and I sat facing my reflection in the mirror. Then there was a brief whirring noise and a recorded voice started to send out instructions.

It seemed that by adjusting various dials I could make my reflection fatter or thinner, change the size of my eyes or nose, try a new eye colour or hairstyle. This was most fun!

I twiddled the reducing knob down to a minimum and a gaunt anorexic me looked back. I lengthened my nose and added gigantic House-of-Windsor ears – freaky!

Next, I decided to treat myself to film star looks – high cheekbones, huge eyes – a wild kind of cat-woman stared back at me!

Then, I gave myself a shorn-off haircut and kind of by accident added quite a bit of chin. This was weirdest of all! I looked like a boy! If I had a brother, I guess he'd look more or less like this. I turned up the skin tone to a delicious shade of tan. Yummy!

Getting well into the spirit of the thing, I added hunky shoulders and a nice set of biceps . . .

I was having a high old time when the machine started to make more whirring noises and the recorded voice said, 'The demonstration is coming to an end. Please select from the Exit options: Erase, Switch, or Copy and Keep. Thank you. Have a good day.'

It seemed a crime to Erase such a seriously divine creature as I'd created.

So I tried Copy and Keep.

The screen kind of 'pixilated' all over and then returned to normal.

I waited, nothing happened.

I hesitated and then I pressed Switch.

The screen pixilated again and in place of the hunk I found my own reflection staring back at me.

And then something very, very odd happened.

I know you're not going to believe this but . . .

My reflection *got up and walked out of the booth.*

I sat for a moment stunned, staring at the screen which was now totally blank.

I was just taking stock of this bi-*zarre* state of affairs when I noticed that there was one hell of a stampede going on outside. In fact, come to think of it, wasn't that a fire alarm?

The curtain of the booth was thrown open.

'You deaf or something?' said the security man. 'You'd better get moving. We're evacuating the whole place. There's a bomb alert.'

Outside people were shouting panicky things about not panicking but everyone was panicking all the same and I was caught up in a huge crush to get out. Before I could think what to do I found I was being carried along in this massive tidal wave of people who were heading towards sets of emergency doors which had been thrown open to let us out.

Quite suddenly we were all outside in the fresh air.

Policemen with megaphones were telling everyone to move across to the other side of the road, which we did.

I elbowed my way through the crowd. I could hear my heart pounding like mad in my chest.

Then through the throng of people, thankfully, I caught sight of Chuck.

'Chuck,' I gasped. I was out of breath, the panic of the whole thing seemed to have made something dreadful happen to my voice.

'Chuck,' I brayed again.

Chuck paused, looked over his shoulder, stared at me blankly, then turned and walked on.

I ran up to him and caught him by the arm.

'Slow down!' I gasped.

'Hang on,' said Chuck as he swung round. 'What the hell do you think you're playing at.'

'Chuck . . .' I wheezed.

'Sorry but . . . Look mate, do I know you?' said Chuck. I think he must have been kind of shell-shocked by the mass panic or something, because he was behaving in the most peculiar fashion.

'For Chryssake, Chuck!' I said.

'Let go! Leave me alone! Who are you?'

I was starting to wonder if he'd had a brainstorm or something.

'Look mate, are you on your own, or did you come with someone?' He seemed to be casting around as if looking for anyone willing to take responsibility for me.

'I came with you!'

Chuck stared at me in a very curious manner.

In a kind of reflex action I brushed my hair out of my eyes, except it wasn't in my eyes. Chryst what had happened to my hair! I felt the back of it . . . it had . . . *gone!* I stared down at my cowboy boots, they weren't too small any more they were *vast.* I worked my way up my jeans . . . *Geesus!*

Two

So that's how I became a boy. Temporarily I mean – at least Chryst! I hope so! As you can see, basically it was all a terrible mistake.

It took forever to convince Chuck of what had happened. I had to buy him three cappuccinos in this really gross Italian café in the North End Road while we went over the whole thing umpteen times.

To start with, he obviously thought I was some loony or freak or tripping on acid or something. In fact, considering it all, he was quite sympathetic. He kind of tried to humour me. He kept on suggesting that we should ring someone and ask them to come and pick me up. As if I had a keeper or something.

Then I really threw him. I rattled off every single fact I could think of that I'd ever known about me . . . about him . . . about the people we knew: telephone numbers, addresses, occupations of parents, size of underwear, the last three movies we'd been to see, the name of his long-defunct tortoise, the number and type of his swimming badges, our GCSE grades, you name it . . .

All through this he was sitting there looking at me with that gaze of blank non-comprehension gorillas have in the zoo. And I was getting more and more mental with the sheer frustration of the whole thing.

'I mean, what have I got to say to convince you, man?' I finished. 'I'm *me* – Justine. I know I don't look like me because incredible as it seems I've been . . . alternativized, changed, transformed, switched! But inside I'm still *me*. Justine – a girl – the one who came here with you. Let's go through it one more time. Look, I met you outside at three-thirty. You were going to bring Alex with you. And I was meant to bring Franz . . .'

Chuck gazed deep into his cappuccino as if enlightenment might dawn like the hand of God appearing through the froth, then he said, 'Look, I don't know who set you up to this. But frankly, I didn't come here this afternoon to sit around with some nutcase faking an identity crisis. So, let's cool it, call it a day. Sorted – OK. Joke over.'

'No wait honestly. I don't know what I can say to make you believe me. Listen, I-dee-gi-a-de-gam-Justi-gus-tini-gi-inige-Du-de-gu-Val-de-gee-You-de-goo-a-de-gar-Chudi-duck.'

He looked up with a kind of weird growing recognition.

'Double-English . . .' he said. 'But it's not on. This kind of thing is strictly beyond the cred–barrier!'

'What if I came out with something only you and me could possibly know?'

'Like what?' he said.

'Like . . .' I paused to give what I was about to say due emphasis. 'Like what happened that time in your father's shed . . .'

Chuck went quite pink and hot.

'But. We swore we wouldn't tell a soul . . .'

I leaned forward and whispered.

'OK,' he said. 'I believe you.'

'So, what the hell am I going to do about it?' I asked.

'Tell me exactly how it happened?' he said.

I explained about the Alternative Reality demo. Chuck made me go through everything in detail. Then I had to describe step by step exactly what the exit options were.

'And what happened after you pressed Copy and Keep?'

'Nothing – so I pressed Switch.'

He let out a low whistle.

'That explains it then,' he said at last. 'You've switched yourself into an Alternative Reality.'

'You mean this isn't really happening?' I said.

'Not really – only virtually. You just think it is. Like the space race.'

'So I can easily get back to normal,' I said.

'Sure,' said Chuck. 'No hassle. You just have to get into that booth and switch yourself back. In fact the sooner the better.'

Chuck and I had a little contretemps after that. He seemed to think that it would be a good idea if I hotfooted it straightaway into Olympia and got myself swopped back again – like right now.

I wasn't so sure. I was starting to see the potential of the situation. As a girl you waste at least half your life fruitlessly trying to fathom out what lurks deep in the masculine psyche. (If anything.) Suddenly, I had been handed a real opportunity to find out what makes the male of the species tick. This was my chance to get some real insider knowledge. I mean why *do* such incredibly naff things as angora jumpers and thigh-high boots turn them on?

But Chuck was insistent.

'For Chryssake. You might get stuck like this. Like for life!'

Reluctantly, I admitted he had a point there. It was a pretty grisly prospect. So I followed him sheepishly back to the exhibition.

By this time the whole place was cordoned off with tapes. Loads of squad cars were blocking the road that led down to Hammersmith Broadway.

A policeman with a loud hailer was directing the last stragglers towards the tube station.

Chuck went up to him and tapped him on the sleeve.

'Is there any chance of us getting back inside?' he asked.

'Not tonight, sonny. Whole place has been sealed off. Left something in there, have you?'

'Well, kind of . . .' said Chuck.

'Not to worry,' he said. 'If there's any lost property our chaps should hand it in. Just report it at your local station.'

'But . . .' said Chuck.

'Now move along now.' And he went back to loud-hailing like mad at a group of kids who had gathered round a TV Outside Broadcast Van.

'Well, I guess there's nothing to do but wait till tomorrow,' I said.

'Wait till tomorrow. Chryst!' said Chuck. 'Honestly I don't know how you're taking this all so calmly!'

I tried very patiently to point out to Chuck the upside of the whole business.

'This is the chance of a lifetime. Imagine how much a girl can learn from an experience like this.'

'What are you suggesting? Writing your memoirs and selling them to the tabloids. My life as a male by Justine Duval?'

'Look, think of it as a unique scientific experiment if you like.'

'OK,' said Chuck. 'So where do we go from here? Say you toddle off home. Has it occurred to you that your parents might just notice something about you is *different*? Or were you thinking of turning up in drag?'

'No problem. I'm staying over at Franz's.'

'You won't be safe!' he said.

'You've got a point there,' I said. 'Better cancel. I'll ring her and say I've changed my mind.'

'Then what?'

'Couldn't I stay at your place?'

'We've turned the spare room into a darkroom,' said Chuck.

'But if I'm just another guy your mother won't mind if I stay in your room.'

'I wouldn't have minded before,' said Chuck.

'Open to a bribe?'

'It depends what . . .'

'Say I get Franz to let you come with us to her parents' place in the South of France next summer?'

'Do you think you could?'

'I can give it a try.'

'All right . . . I suppose maybe it'll be OK. Just for one night . . .' he said grudgingly.

I instinctively leaned over and threw an arm round him.

'Cool it,' he said. 'Geesus. For a moment I thought you were going to kiss me or something. From now on, remember, keep your distance!'

So we headed off in search of a phone. I was concentrating pretty hard on taking masculine strides.

I think I must have got the hang of this because I couldn't help noticing the way girls were looking at me – shameless hussies!

When a male eyes a girl, he just kind of gives her a quick once-over and then moves on. But these girls! They'd look you straight in the eye until you looked away. Even women old enough to know better, a lot better, kind of *noticed* me.

And then I caught sight of myself full-length in a shop window and realized why.

Boy! There was no doubt about it. I hardly like to say this for fear of sounding vain. But here was quite some hunk.

I lingered to admire my reflection.

Meanwhile, Chuck had located a phone booth. He was signalling violently at me to hurry.

'You'd better let me do the talking,' he said. He was already dialling the number.

'Why?'

'Your voice!'

'Hi, Franz.'

'Hello.'

'It's me, Chuck.'

'I know. Have you got Alex with you?'

'No.'

'Do you know where he is?'

'No I don't.'

'Well, if you do see him, could you please *not* tell him that you spoke to me this afternoon? Just say I wasn't in?'

'Just like that? Won't he think that rather odd?'

'I want him to think I was out, that's all.'

'But you're not.'

Chuck was being incredibly dense, so I kicked him.

'Just agree. OK?' I whispered in his ear.

'Who's that?' demanded Franz.

'No one.'

'It's Alex, isn't it.'

'No it's not. It's Justine.'

'Let me speak to her then,' said Franz, suspicion surfacing in her voice.

'A bit difficult at the moment,' said Chuck, 'I'm running out of coins. Listen she just wants me to tell you that she can't stay at your place tonight OK?'

'Oh I see,' said Franz and then, enlightenment suddenly dawning, she added, 'Well, take care!'

Chuck put down the receiver with a sigh.

'Now look what you've done. She thinks we're *going out* together.'

'You must be joking!' I said. Then catching sight of Chuck's face I realized the tactless nature of the comment.

So I added, 'Well, it's not as if we fancy each other or anything.'

Which I suppose made it worse.

'Not right now, we don't,' said Chuck and thrust his hands in his pockets and started walking ahead of me.

I followed thoughtfully, taking stock of the situation. It looked as if for the moment I had landed myself with a whole new persona. For tonight at any rate. And as luck would have it, tonight was Saturday night – there was no better time to carry out a little research into what went on behind enemy lines.

I realize now that at the time I didn't take any of this particularly seriously. I mean the whole thing was so unbelievable. It was more like having an incredibly vivid dream that you just go along with to see what will happen next. But while it lasted I was going to make full use of it. I was going to exploit this opportunity to the hilt and find out as much as I could about what it was like to be on the other side of the sexual divide.

It wasn't until later that I started to investigate all those deeper issues. Like what makes males think they are brighter, braver, better at fixing things. Why males always consider themselves more in control, more objective, less silly, less shallow – as they see it, basically better material. How they manage to claim that they never gossip or cry or sulk and *how*, so infuriatingly, males can get away with thinking they're *always right*.

★

Anyway to get back to *virtual* reality. It was around six when we left Olympia. This meant we had four hours to kill before any real action started – so we decided to head back to Chuck's place for a shower and to recharge the batteries.

That journey to Chuck's home was my first experience of seeing the world through masculine eyes.

You know, I'd always had this innocent little theory that, first and foremost, we're all people – whether we happen to be male or female is a matter of small, although not insignificant, physical differences. There are, of course, those deep formative cultural influences like whether you were given a Sindy doll or an Action Man to model yourself on. But, basically, up until that Saturday night, I used to think that underneath we were all pretty much the same kind of animal.

Well, I'm telling you now for a fact. This is definitely *not* so. What I soon discovered is that we are utterly – I mean utterly and totally – different.

For a start, imagine what it's like suddenly to gain four stone – just like that – most of it, I'm glad to say, in solid muscle. Striding out of Olympia, I felt like a cross between Superman and the Jolly Green Giant.

But what was more amazing was that the world looked different – apart from being a lot lower down, I mean. Something most peculiar seemed to have happened to my eyesight. I found myself automatically picking out all the different makes of cars that passed – and even the motorbikes. All of a sudden, I could tell a Yamaha from a Suzuki. I mean, I've never really bothered to look twice at a motorbike before.

We came to a halt at a bus stop. The bus stop was situated bang in front of a chemist's shop. I stared absentmindedly into the window and was confronted by mind-blowing acres of naked female flesh. There were all these females staring at me with that particular 'come-hither-but-don't-touch' look models have. That's when it struck me that the whole window – in fact the whole shop – was utterly stuffed, packed, jammed – positively oozing femininity. The only corner males got a tiny look in was one apologetic display of Cossack Hair Gel and Deodorant, crushed in between the stacks of Bikini Bare and Born Blonde. And they call it a man's world!

Then, in the bus, I found everything had shrunk. I had to stoop my way down the aisle like a hunchback. Chuck seemed to be happy to stand in this cramped position but I caught sight of an empty seat and, folding myself in two, I thankfully manoeuvred my body into it. There was just about enough room to sit with my knees wedged apart by the back of the seat in front. The woman sharing my seat twitched her coat from under me and shifted her buttocks over giving me a deeply distrustful look. Then she flapped out her *Evening Standard* and returned to reading it. In order to get my own back I started ostentatiously to read her paper over her shoulder.

RAPE – Shock New Statistics

the headline glared back at me – accusingly.

Just as I was deep into the third column of hair-raising evidence and shocking statistics about how it's practically impossible not to get raped if you're a female foolhardy enough to risk further education – I found Chuck was shaking me by the shoulder. We had reached his stop and it was time to get off.

As we headed down the street to Chuck's house something occurred to me.

'What are we going to tell your parents?' I asked, suddenly wondering what it would be like to be face to face with Maggie – Chuck's mother.

Chuck shrugged.

'We'd better cook up some story about where you've come from.'

Actually, it might have been better if we'd thought of this earlier because at that moment I heard a shrill:

'Coooeee!'

The originator of this familiar nesting cry came staggering across the pavement with a load of bulging Tesco bags.

'Thank goodness I saw you. I got carried away and bought far too much,' Maggie panted.

She unloaded her bags on to us without so much as a 'Do you mind?'.

'Who's this?' she said brightly.

'This?' said Chuck. 'Oh this is, er . . . Jake.'

'Hi,' said Maggie without so much as a hint of recognition.

'Hi,' I replied, feeling really odd. I mean Maggie has known me from birth – before virtually.

'Is it all right if Jake stays the night?'

'Fine!' she said. Then added for my benefit, 'As long as you can stand the chaos.'

By the time we had gone the hundred or so yards down the road to Chuck's house, Maggie had already carried out a major inquisition into my origins, marital status, social standing, dental records etc. during which time Chuck had established: that my parents were abroad; that I was meant to be staying with another friend, but he'd got mumps so I couldn't – the final straw came as Maggie opened the front door and asked 'Whereabouts?'

'Clapham.'

'No, I mean whereabouts are your parents?'

My mind went blank. I cast a pleading glance at Chuck.

It just so happened that at that point Chuck had taken a leaflet about using recycled loo paper to save the world's endangered species out of the top of Maggie's shopping basket.

'Mauritius,' he said.

We dumped the Tesco bags in the kitchen and headed upstairs as quickly as possible.

'Why on earth did you say Mauritius?' I demanded when we were safely behind Chuck's closed bedroom door.

'It's the only place I could think of that my parents don't know anything about. At least I hope not.'

'Nor do I!' I objected.

'Anyway, I thought it might account for your accent.'

'What accent?'

'Mansard Drawl,' said Chuck. 'You know – the way you Mansard Hall lot talk, finishing off all the words like foreigners. None of my friends talk like that. She'd smell a rat.'

'I don't know what you mean, finishing off our words?' I objected.

Chuck sighed.

'Do you want to shower first or shall I?'

While Chuck showered I took the opportunity to take a good look round his room. Geesus, what a tip!

As a girl, you kind of keep updating yourself. The key moves from Winnie-the-Pooh to Laura Ashley, on to pop posters then into framed art prints and black satin sheets, all mark vital stages in one's formative development. A male just doesn't seem to care. In fact, by the look of it Chuck had simply never moved on to, or from, anything. He had just left everything as it was and added to it until all the material from his past had accumulated in layers. Now it was kind of mulching down like a compost heap.

I picked my way across the floor to the bunk beds. Chuck's duvet cover still bore the print, well-washed but still in all its faded glory, of a circa 1985 high performance car.

Since the main storage area for clothes appeared to be the floor, I was curious to see what was in the wardrobe. I opened the door and most of Chuck's past leapt out at me. Cricket bat, pads, skateboard, seriously outgrown roller skates, mossy-looking jumpers, masses and masses of books with lurid jackets and titles like *Rats, Fog* and *Plague* and a collection of dating 'vinyl' in dog-eared sleeves. I shoved as much as I could back into the wardrobe and continued. Nosing their way through the dust on the windowsill I came across a sad little convoy of Chuck's Airfix vintage model cars which led to a corner of the room – an area which was comparatively tidy by Chuck standards – inhabited by his computer. It stood on a 'shelving system' which was a monument to the tenacity of DIY. It leaned in all directions at once, the main form of support being carefully stacked cassettes – heaven knows what happened when he wanted to play them.

Finishing my tour of inspection I returned to his bed. Beside it, roughly painted with matt black paint, and covered in half-scraped-off turtle transfers, was an old 'thirties bedside table with a drawer.

I wasn't really snooping – just trying to get the drawer to shut properly. It only had letters in it anyway and some cards, most of which I couldn't help noticing were somehow familiar. And there was an envelope with photos in it . . .

As it happened, I featured in quite a few of them. They weren't very good ones, actually. I couldn't even remember when some of them were taken . . .

I could hear Chuck coming back so I shoved the drawer in guiltily.

'Looking for something?' he asked.

'Pyjamas.'

'I think there's a spare pair in the chest of drawers.'

Chuck had come in wearing nothing but his 501s. I think he was trying to look like the guy in the Levi's ad. It's hard to tell because Chuck is not over-endowed with muscle. He also has a pretty fair skin and would never dream of going near a sunbed, so, apart from the jeans, the resemblance could best be described as distant.

The chest of drawers was so effectively camouflaged by photos of the Doors that I hadn't even noticed it.

I found some in the top drawer. As I lifted them out, lying underneath was a very worn and limp woolly sheep.

'What's this?' I asked.

Chuck paused from rubbing his hair with a towel.

'Oh, that's a sheep,' he said. Clearly any hope of looking macho was rapidly receding.

'Honestly Chuck, you can't keep this old thing.' I lifted it out. 'Look, it's falling apart.'

'That's Meredith,' he said. And he added with obvious restraint, 'Would you mind putting her back please?'

Then it was my turn for a shower. OK no sniggering – we all know what little boys are made of. Actually it's amazing how quickly you can get used to being – how can I put it – *different*. I mean the Davises only had a very small mirror in their bathroom and it kept misting up so I could only see myself in bits – which maybe shielded me somewhat from a full confrontation.

But, actually, instead of thinking *gross* I came to the conclusion that I was 'rather sweet' as a matter of fact. A medium-toasted tan, good shoulders, flat stomach, amazingly hairy legs, maybe a bit too much chin.

I rubbed a space clear in the mirror and examined my face.

Oh my god, that surely couldn't be a spot! I mean this was serious, man! No chance of a camouflage job. I flung a mega-dose of aftershave on it which made it redder.

Then I climbed on the bathroom scales – between my two enormous feet the dial showed 11 stone 2lb. Impressive!

Standing back from the mirror, I tried to make a precise assessment of my rating – from the sex appeal point of view.

I was distracted from this important consideration by a another high 'Coooee,' from below.

'Supper time! Anyone hungry?' came Maggie's voice.

I put the shower on full and flung myself into it.

Three

I've always been rather intrigued by Chuck's parents. I mean, they must account for a lot of the way Chuck's turned out. There can't be that much difference in age between my parents and his. But, despite their age, my parents are totally normal.

My father is everything you'd expect a father to be — obsessed by News and Weather, paranoid about Locks, Lights and Telephone Bills, and literally suicidal about the State of the Economy. Little else seems to register with him. Mummy, like most mothers, handles all the things that matter — like Decor, Dinner Parties and Dress Allowances — the reassuring thing about my parents is that their life is totally predictable.

Anyway, Chuck's aren't a bit like that. They're what Mummy calls — with 'that look' of hers — 'Children of the 'Sixties'. The 'Sixties seem to have totally by-passed my parents — while all that free love, drug-slipping and wild behaviour was going on, I think they must have been holed up in a nuclear fall-out shelter or something. But Chuck's parents were caught up in it all and in a funny sense they've stayed that way, as if they were trapped in a time warp. You can tell the minute you meet Maggie. I mean, she can be dressed in absolutely nondescript clothes — a sweater and jeans or something and she'll give herself away with some tiny little touch – like ethnic slippers.

Anyway, basically this is all to prepare you for the culture shock of a meal Chez Davis. The kitchen, as you would predict, is stripped pine – I mean everything's stripped – the furniture, the floor, the door, the window frames – even the little square of wood behind the light switch. It's as if Casper (Chuck's father) had had a sort of mission to purge the world of gloss paint. This fetish has kept him poised like a mass murderer over an acid bath in the garage for most of the last decade. Sad waste of life really when you consider how painted kitchens have made a comeback – Mummy's already on to her second Smallbone.

Maggie indulges her retro leanings by cooking on an ancient Aga – so meals that would occur at regular intervals from some reliable source like a microwave tend to turn up haphazardly at the Davis', as the Aga thinks appropriate.

Anyway, one of these appropriate occasions had arisen while I was in the shower.

I power-showered. I was ravenous.

I arrived downstairs to find the table was laid, we even had a napkin each – admittedly a recycled paper one, but still . . .

'I hope you like black-eyed peas,' said Maggie, doling out a massive portion beside the pile of what looked threateningly like calamari on my plate. 'They're our latest craze.'

As she passed the plate she gave me a smile with just a hint of girlishness about it.

I noticed that she had actually bothered to put on lipstick and a trace of foundation. Now, I'm used to the sleeves-rolled-up, glasses-on, chat-over-a-mug-of-coffee Maggie. As a girl, I had never been given lush treatment like this.

At that point, Casper came in and it suddenly occurred to me that I ought to register his entrance in some way – so I sort of shuffled to my feet to shake him by the hand. The idea even crossed my mind that maybe I ought to call him

'Sir' like boys do when they really want to make a good impression on my father – but I thought better of it and decided to settle for 'Mr Davis' instead. Casper is a school-teacher so he actually revels in being one-of-us. Even calling him 'Mr Davis' is pretty cruel but I thought maybe I'd let him suffer for a while.

Casper shook me by the hand and even gave me a friendly paw-on-shoulder kind of masculine pat, clearly intended to put me in my place.

You know, it didn't really strike me till later, but all through that meal I was kind of trying to impress Casper. Not to get the upper hand exactly, but certainly to make my presence felt. I'd never had to bother as a girl – weird!

We started with a bit of a discussion about the Exhibition which led on to Virtual Reality in general and I found myself expressing, quite forcefully, all sorts of opinions I never knew I'd had before. I got into rather deep water actually.

In fact, it was a pretty uncomfortable meal all round as I kept having to steer the conversation away from Mauritius.

'Tell us something about your parents,' said Maggie. 'What precisely are they doing in Mauritius?'

'Oh they're . . . er . . . farming,' I said.

'How interesting. What sort of things grow there?'

Now this was a tricky question for someone with my grasp of Geography. I mean I wasn't even sure if Mauritius was in the northern or southern hemisphere, let alone which latitude, so I said to be on the safe side, 'Well, it's livestock mainly.'

'Oh really? What kind?'

I sent Chuck a pleading glance. He'd been checking through his *Pears Junior Encyclopedia* while I was in the shower.

Chuck was staring with a concentrated frown down at his plate. There written in calamari was the word 'dodo'.

'Dodos . . .' I said.

There was an awkward silence after this and Chuck looked as if he was going to asphyxiate on a black-eyed pea.

'But surely the dodo is extinct . . .' said Casper.

'Oh they are,' cut in Chuck. 'In the wild. But Jake's father has started this cross-breeding experiment. You know like the zonkie – half-zebra-half-donkey? Well he's been crossing pigeons with a turkey and he's come up with this creature that's virtually identical to a dodo.'

'They're a kind of mock-dodo, like a mock turtle,' I added helpfully.

'Really!' said Casper and started scratching reflectively at some black-eyed pea sauce that had caked itself into his Icelandic handknit. 'What do they breed them for?'

'Umm food, really. To eat, you know. They're going to be the big alternative to turkey – like for Christmas and Thanksgiving – they're vast you see.' I was warming to the subject.

'How amazing,' said Maggie. 'What do they taste like?'

'Well, a bit like goose, less fatty but more kind of gamey.'

'Gosh, imagine serving dodo for Christmas – it sounds kind of sacrilegious somehow.'

'The serving of turkey dates back to a pagan custom,' said Casper.

After that they all got heavily into a discussion about the origin of the Christmas tree, so the pressure was off me.

'So what have you chaps got planned for this evening?' asked Maggie, some time later as she was taking our plates away.

Chuck said he wasn't sure and I waited for the interrogation to continue. But it didn't.

We actually managed to escape from the kitchen without washing up, without giving a full and detailed account of our movements for the night ahead and without even having negotiated a proper curfew time.

'Don't be too late,' was the only guidance given.

Boy! Was this living!

Back in Chuck's room, I lay on the top bunk studying the ceiling. Chuck was down below in the hall getting stuck into negotiations for the evening. It was amazing to have absolutely nothing to do. I mean boys must have so much slack time on their hands!

Normally, around this period of a Saturday night, I'd be deep into the hectic routine of serious body maintenance. Come to think of it, few males do anything to merit the dedicated preparations carried out for their benefit. Four hours of straightening hair, plucking eyebrows, Immac-ing legs, fake-tanning face – meantime safeguarding twenty wet nails (all with the portable phone lodged under one's chin juggling the night's alternatives). Was it worth it, I was asking myself . . .?

I strained my ears to hear what Chuck was plotting on the phone.

His language had switched to telephone mode.

'Yeah sorted, got a mate stacking at my place.'

'......'

'It's OK. He's mental.'

'......'

'Hardcore, not the energetic type. So no rushing, better check out some other venue.'

'......'

'Not on. Rentals won't vacate.'

'......'

'Pukka . . .'

Chuck sauntered into the room and threw himself on to his bunk.

I leaned over and asked, 'What was all that about?'

'We're cool – no hassle. It's sorted. We're going to dock at the G'n B.'

'Then what?'

'Well, first Al suggests Asylum, but it's high on the E scene, got busted last week, so I advise revise sitewise . . .'

'Chuck, do you think you could tone down the dialogue a bit?'

'Sorry, those guys are ravers – serious clubbers. You only get a hearing if you can crack their code.'

'Anyway, why can't we go to Asylum?'

I had been dying to go there. Mummy has always been absolutely paranoid about clubs – I think it has something to do with seeing too many black and white B movies in her youth – she links the whole scene with heavy drinking, loose sex, the criminal underworld and wickedly seductive middle-aged men. Actually, according to my personal experience, you were exposed to much more of that sort of thing at a lunchtime cocktail party in Cheyne Walk. But one way or another 'clubs' had been put strictly out of bounds. However, she could hardly have the veto over my current social life.

'I reckon I've got to keep an eye on you,' said Chuck.

'For Chryssake! What do I have to do to convince you that I'm perfectly capable of looking after myself!?'

By nine-thirty, both nicely marinated in Chuck's Antaeus, we were heading for Hammersmith Broadway tube station. Once in the tube, Chuck was giving me instructions on how not to let him down and I was hoping that we didn't smell *too irresistible* – normally I can handle a certain amount of sexual harassment, but frankly I didn't fancy being mobbed in my current condition.

'You'll drink lager, OK? Sol or Grolsch or something,' said Chuck. 'And for godsake don't ask for a glass! Stick with me and stand at the bar and please – if you must sit down, try not to sit like that or you'll ruin my cred.'

I adjusted my position.

'You'd better have some dosh on you,' said Chuck, taking a fiver out of his pocket and handing it over. 'Now listen carefully – round technique: if you see a female on Southern Comfort and Canada Dry, give her a wide berth until she's got a full glass in her hand – then you can move in. Basically you'd be wisest to stick to the females on Diet Pepsi – they tend to be more controllable too. And don't get stuck with any dogs. If you get sidetracked with a girl who's plain as sin by all means talk to her, but they tend to cling like grim death if you exhibit too much sympathy. The art of the whole thing is to breeze, man.'

It was a hell of a lot to take in. I was starting to look at Chuck with rather more respect than usual. Mind you, I'd never actually noticed him 'breezing' in the past. I remembered him more as propping up the bar on his own and then being left there when we all moved on.

The pub we were meant to be meeting Chuck's friends at was in the Fulham Road. By the time we got there most of the people were standing outside on the pavement. Which was odd really because it wasn't particularly full inside. Chuck and I had sort of slunk up to it with our hands in our pockets and Chuck had zoomed inside to see if his friends has arrived, and they hadn't. So he instructed me on how to lean cowboy-fashion against the wall outside and look cool. Then he reached in his pocket and brought out a packet of Marlboro.

'But you don't smoke,' I hissed.

Chuck gave me a withering glance and dragged on his fag with a look of concentration.

A load of Mansard Hall girls went past – fourth years – they said 'Hi' to Chuck and gave me lightning head to crutch assessment.

I could see one of them giggling and whispering something in the next girl's ear.

God, HATE VIBES – I had developed this sudden and

pronounced loathing for girls who giggled. Did I ever giggle? I wondered.

A load more boys turned up and kept shooting into the bar looking around and then shooting out again. Nobody seemed to say much or drink anything and a lot of cigarettes were passed around. Occasionally one of these forays was rewarded by a chorus of shrieks and a certain amount of kissing of a fairly platonic nature. Once greeted, the guys would come out and resume hanging around outside.

'Aren't we going to have a drink?' I asked after a while. I was getting cold actually.

'Wait till that lot have settled in,' said Chuck. 'Otherwise you'll have to stand the lot of them a round and that'll totally clean us out.'

At last Chuck raised an eyebrow and I followed him, thankfully, inside.

The bar was flanked by a load of absolutely massive blokes. I think they must have been a rugby team or something. They were getting pretty rowdy and swigging down pints of beer and making a hell of a lot of noise. Chuck elbowed his way through and came back with two bottles of lager and we stood crushed up against a corner of the bar with a view mainly of vast expanses of tracksuited backsides. One bloke, who was particularly obnoxious and whose tracksuit bottoms kind of slipped at the back giving a glimpse of a cleave between giant buttocks, kept stepping back and guffawing. The third time he trod on my foot, I sort of accidentally leaned back against him and his beer slopped a bit.

'So sorry,' I said.

'Cancha-watch wha ya garn,' he slurred.

'I beg your pardon?' I said.

'Trying ta be funny?'

'I just didn't quite catch . . .'

At that moment someone elbowed me and with a sort of

inevitable chain-reaction Bum-Cleave's beer got slopped again.

Bum-Cleave glowered.

I think Chuck had had enough of this because at that point he headed off to the Gents signalling violently for me to follow.

Which I did – and regretted. Just as I thought – it was GROSS! So I hurriedly backed out searching around for some safe retreat. I spied a seat conveniently empty near the Mansard Hall girls.

'Excuse me, is this taken?'

'No it's free, actually.' The look which came back at me from under her fringey eyelashes was of the blatant come-hither variety.

So I sat down.

Six pairs of Mansard Hall eyes confronted me.

What on earth do guys say in this situation?

'Anyone like a drink?' I asked, just praying that they wouldn't all say yes.

Fringey Lashes was obviously intent on keeping me clamped to the seat, so she said: 'No, we're fine actually.'

I gazed at my lager.

'Are you with those chaps over there?' Fringey asked, indicating the rugby louts who had joined arms and were having a kind of impromptu scrum against the bar.

'No, why?'

'They keep looking over here and talking about you.'

'Oh yeah,' I said and sank further into Chuck's Levi jacket.

It was at that moment that I felt a presence towering over me.

The Mansard Hall girls responded with a nervous group-titter.

'I think ya sittin in ma seat,' said a voice. It was Bum-Cleave. He was leaning over me at a forty-five degree angle.

'I don't think so . . .' I started.

Bum-Cleave's beer could withstand the force of gravity no longer. It started to trickle into my lap. I leaped to my feet.

'That's ma like it,' said Bum-Cleave sliding into my seat and putting an arm round Fringey.

'Look here . . .' I said.

Fringey looked at Bum-Cleave in disgust and, with the clarity of tone born of a good private education, stated the blindingly obvious.

'I think you're drunk,' she said. 'And I think you're being obnoxious.'

'So do I,' I said supportively.

'Yer-what,' said Bum-Cleave, rising to his feet again.

'I said I think you're drunk . . . and . . .'

'And . . .?' B-C was sticking his face into mine so that I could feel the damp heat of his breath on my skin.

'And you're being . . .'

'Ob-nox-i-ous,' he said, spelling out each syllable. 'Afta me now . . . ob . . . nox . . .'

I had hardly been aware that I had been backing inexorably towards the doors of the pub. It was unfortunate that, at the very moment Bum-Cleave pushed me, Chuck, who had emerged from the Gents, had grasped the situation and headed out through one set of doors and then raced full speed round the pub to this particular set. And opened them . . . So I fell flat on my back on the pavement and Bum-Cleave, wrong-footed by my sudden descent, fell heavily on top of me.

'**** me,' said Bum-Cleave.

This neatly coincided with Chuck's friends turning up. I looked up from the pavement and found I was surrounded by a reassuring array of Stussy sweatshirts. Chuck's friends were VAST, which was convenient, because they had quite a job on their hands. They heaved Bum-Cleave off me and propped him against the wall. This left me lying on the ground gasping for breath and wondering if I'd broken my back. I don't think I could have done because once they'd picked me up and dusted me down I actually found I could stagger. Fortunate, because Bum-Cleave's mates were pouring through the doors by then, and it just so happened – with one of those rare flukes of fortune that so seldom occur when you basically need them – that a Number 14 bus was heading up the road towards us. So we all kind of fell on to it.

Four

So this is how I happened to be on a 14 bus heading for Piccadilly with a massive bruise on the back of my head, dirt all down my back and beer all down the front of my jeans so that it looked as if I'd pissed myself.

By the time the bus reached Piccadilly, I had got my breath back.

It appeared that one of the guys, whose name was Matt, had a birthday that day. He was sixteen so this obviously called for 'congratulations' and boy! – couldn't fellas be specific when it came to what he could now add to his legally acceptable activities!

But anyway, apart from the numerous *small* gifts, one of the boys had brought along a parcel carefully wrapped in kitchen foil. He passed it over to Matt with a wink and slap on the shoulder.

Inside was a rather flat home-baked cake.

'Birthday cake! Rigid Cool! Muchas!' said Matt.

I was touched. I mean, at school we girls normally batch-bake for each other's birthdays so that we can all pig out on cake and skip the mandatory grease-bowl at lunchtime. But to picture this guy – who looked pretty ferocious actually – rolling up his sleeves and baking a birthday cake for his friend . . . Well, frankly, it almost redeemed my faith in the male gender.

'OK,' said Matt. 'Off Hold and Scan In, Man.'

He broke off little bits of cake and handed them round.

It was scrummy. Kind of like a massive soft-bake chocolate chip cookie. Sharing the cake seemed to revive everyone's spirits. A boy called Fozzy was cracking jokes that had us all falling about. In fact, I'd even started to forget about the bruise on the back of my head. And after all, even if I had got beer all down the front of my jeans – who cared!?

A couple of the boys had got out fags and were smoking surreptitiously, holding them cupped in their hands. We were all feeling pretty chilled and matey when . . .

The bus conductor, who must have had a smoke alarm for a nose, shot up the stairs and looked around suspiciously. He rang the bell twice and the bus shuddered to a halt.

'OK, so who's been smoking?' he demanded. 'This bus isn't moving till we find out.'

Somewhere in the midst of this, I found that the cake had been thrust into my hands to hold. So while the discussion went on with the conductor as to whether or not anyone had been smoking or whether it was just the general niffiness of the bus, and whether this might or might not be an appropriate place to chuck us all off it, I had been nibbling at the little bits that kept crumbling off in my hand.

I have to confess that I'm a real pig about cookies – especially like this one, which had really massive chocolate chips and loads of kind of coconutty bits. The more I ate, the more delicious it tasted. You know one of the great unrecognized advantages of being male is that one's major paranoid concern in life has been lifted – you don't care a damn about putting on weight.

Anyway, meanwhile, a lot of the other bus passengers joined in the row, and so, with a typical triumph of official-dom over the freedom of the individual, we were callously ordered down the stairs and out into the cold night air. The Number 14 took off, leaving us stranded in Shaftesbury Avenue.

'Chryst,' said Matt. 'The cake!'

'It's OK. I've got it!' I said.

I handed it over.

'Geesus. Where's it all blown?' he said.

I felt a bit guilty but, quite honestly, I thought he was getting a bit heavy about a silly old birthday cake, after all there was still quite a bit left.

He broke it into crumbs and shared them around, intentionally leaving me out this time.

'Head start,' said Al, when he'd licked the foil clean. 'Let's move to Asylum before they shred the guest list.'

~

Luckily, Chuck seemed to have forgotten his misgivings about taking me to this particularly 'mental' club. In fact, he seemed in an uncharacteristically carefree mood. He swung round a couple of lamp-posts vaulted over three conveniently placed Soho rubbish bags and stumbled off at a kind of ambling trot.

We had to foot it through the Soho back streets to get to the club. I thought once or twice about what Mummy would have said if she had known that I was loose in this '*hotbed-of-vice*'. Actually, it all looked disappointingly tame to me; the only really suspicious-looking characters turned out to be a group of Japanese tourists who'd surrounded a policeman in order to have their photo taken with him.

Anyway, by the time we reached Asylum there were two queues stretching halfway down the street. The guest-list queue was, if anything, longer than the standard payment queue. So we joined the standard one with the aim of swopping over when we got to the head of it.

I was feeling pretty euphoric by this time. This was the life

– the freedom of the city with the fully paid-up option to stay out all night long – the company of a group of guys who weren't bent on chatting me up – or sending me up – but who were just being nice and matey – and the luxury (without having to make the least effort in the world) of knowing I looked, although I say it myself, pretty wicked.

A fact that had been noticed by the group of girls ahead of us in the queue.

'You ask him then,' I heard one say.

'No you . . .' followed by a stifled giggle.

There was a lot of to-ing and fro-ing about who was going to ask whatever it was and then one of the girls leaned in my direction and said with mind-blowing originality 'Got a light?'

'Sorry, don't smoke . . .' I said.

'You in training?' the first girl went on, eyeing me up and down.

'No, just scared it'll stunt my growth,' I said, trying to be as offhand as possible.

'OOOOH!' screamed the girls as if this was the most killingly funny thing anyone had ever said. 'How tall are you anyway?'

'Six foot three when he's not in heels,' said Fozzy.

And the girls thought this was even funnier.

I tried to ignore their presence as there followed a long discussion about my exact height. And the girl who had done all the talking stood back to back with me and kind of wriggled her body against mine.

I cast pleading glances at Chuck.

But he was in a particularly unsympathetic mood and, along with the others, he had started egging the girls on.

In fact, all the boys were really getting into the spirit of it and in an easily overheard undertone they were giving the girls the low-down on me. It seemed that, among other things, I had been selected as striker for England, but had turned the offer down as I was afraid I might get injured and it'd spoil my filming career – but frankly, I didn't have to work anyway because my Dad owned most of Belgravia. (Modesty prevents me revealing more.) *I could have killed them!*

By the time we reached the head of the queue, the girls were gazing at me as if I were giving off clouds of stardust.

I was saved by the bouncer on the door.

'OK, we'll take you lot,' he said to the girls. 'But we're not letting all them in.'

And the girls shot through the door with a shriek and a wave and a 'See you inside then!'

'Why not?' demanded Al.

'Club's full,' said the bouncer. 'From now on every bloke has to be accompanied.'

'But we are accompanied,' said Chuck. 'By each other.'

'Accompanied means with a girl, see,' said the bouncer.

'No, I don't see,' said Chuck. 'They weren't accompanied.'

'They were girls . . .'

'That's sexual discrimination,' said Matt. 'That's illegal.'

'Anyway we're on the guest list,' said Fozzy.

And just in the nick of time, as we were about to be sent to the back of the guest-list queue, Fozzy's friend – who'd put us on the list in the first place – materialized through the smoke-filled atmosphere and stood in the doorway – a heaven-sent apparition in all-black leather-gear.

So, quite suddenly, we found ourselves inside.

We eased our way in through the bodies monopolizing the dance floor and, having located the bar through the smoke, fought our way towards it, battling against the force of the sound waves. The atmosphere was like a sauna turned on maximum.

I was stooping, partly so that I could find air to breathe,

but mainly so that I wouldn't get noticed by our 'friends' from the queue. But I needn't have worried really. The place was so dark and the laser lights were so dazzling that it was virtually impossible to recognize anyone.

Actually, they were playing some pretty amazing music. One of the boys handed me a Grolsch and we all started dancing in a kind of manic way. In fact, I think quite a few people apart from me enjoyed the cooling benefit of my Grolsch. My hands had started making some fairly uncontrollable flapping actions.

It must have been really good music because I soon had the distinct impression that my feet were no longer actually in touch with the floor. I was flying somewhere near ceiling level and everyone was staring upwards watching me with a mixture of amazement and admiration. It was round about then that I realized something was very, very wrong . . .

My heart was pounding in my chest like a pile driver. And everyone's face had begun to ooze into everyone else's until they looked like a terrible uncoordinated slur of primordial swamp people.

I don't know how I made it to the door. I just knew I had to get outside because if I was going to die I wanted to do it in the fresh air. I might well have crawled there for all I could remember.

In fact, from then on, I totally lost the next five hours or so and I would never have known what had happened if I hadn't forced Chuck to tell me when I came round, laid out on his bunk, at about five-thirty the next morning.

According to Chuck's reconstruction, I must have been sitting on the pavement outside for quite a long time before the girls we'd met in the queue found me there.

'Geesus,' I said. 'Not the ones who were chatting me up?'

Chuck nodded. 'But I don't think you'll be bothered by them again.'

'Why's that? I wasn't violent or anything, was I?'

'Not exactly,' said Chuck.

'Well, what happened then?'

'Well, to tell the truth, you were sitting on the pavement er . . .'

'Er . . . what?'

'Crying . . . and . . .'

'And . . .?'

Chuck cleared his throat: 'You kept saying that you wanted . . . hh . . . hm "Mummy".'

I was silent for a moment while this sank in.

All in all I have recorded the date of this event for posterity as the very worst and most humiliating night of my life. Chuck had been an absolute star. He had been simply livid when he realized what Fozzy had put in the cake.

Apparently he had stood on the pavement ranting on about what irresponsible, certifiable idiots they all were, then he bundled me in a taxi and took me home. When I started coming round, I felt so ill I wanted to die. I spent half the time flying around the ceiling of Chuck's bedroom and the other half with my head down the loo.

As if I hadn't suffered enough, the following morning, which was a Sunday, was pretty bad news too.

As dawn broke, I managed to stagger downstairs. I was past the hot flushes stage and into the cold shivery bit and all I could think of was getting a hot cup of tea inside me. I groped round the kitchen like a zombie reaching for things by touch – I mean, I knew Chuck's kitchen like the back of my hand. In fact better, considering the way the backs of my hands had been behaving of late.

All the time I was trying to make the tea, I was being watched by Stalin who was sitting on the Davis' stripped pine rocking chair and staring at me with a knowing look in his deep yellow eyes.

(It's OK, I know what you're thinking, but as a matter of fact, Stalin is the Davis' cat.)

Suddenly, Stalin made a bolt for the back door and shot out through the cat flap.

Casper entered the kitchen.

'Puss . . . puss . . . puss,' he said, ineffectually.

Stalin glared through the kitchen window, arched his back and hissed.

Casper sighed.

'Sorry about the cat,' he said. 'Can't stand people. Some brute probably maltreated the poor little devil – nice to see you up early!'

I nodded into my tea and wondered if I could risk saying anything without it coming out as gobbledegook.

'God knows I've tried . . .' continued Casper on the subject of the cat. 'About the only person he responds to is Maggie . . . and a friend of Chuck's, Justine.'

I swallowed a huge mouthful of tea at the mention of *my* name.

'You know Justine?' asked Casper.

'Eeerwellumm . . . kind' ov,' I said.

Casper took out a tin-opener, opened a tin of cat food and scooped some out on to a saucer which he placed invitingly near the cat flap.

Stalin glared at it through the window but didn't move so much as a whisker. For a cat who'd spent the night enforcing his reign of terror over the neighbourhood, he was showing remarkable restraint.

'Puss . . .' called Casper and, then hearing the distant

sound of a newspaper sliding through the letterbox, shuffled off in his slippers to get it.

By the time Casper returned, Stalin had polished off the cat food and was sitting on my lap purring like a pneumatic drill.

Perhaps I should explain – like practically everything else in the Davis' house, Stalin is recycled. The family had reclaimed him from a home for abandoned cats and Maggie and I had spent hours together feeding him with a finger dipped in cat food until he was strong enough to eat properly. It seemed, despite my new 'image', that Stalin could still recognize his recent benefactor. He was showing his undying gratitude in no uncertain terms.

'Good Lord,' said Casper. 'You've certainly got a way with animals.'

'Anything in the paper?' I asked, in an attempt to divert Casper's attention from Stalin who was licking my neck.

Casper eased himself into a chair and opened his *Sunday Independent*. 'Tsk . . . tsk . . . tsk': he made disapproving tutting noises.

I leaned over and displayed an intelligent interest in the headlines:

Bomb destroys 3 million worth of hi-tech exhibits

Beneath these words was a photograph. Amid the tangled mass of wreckage, I could distinguish the corner of something that looked familiar. It looked very much like the corner of an upturned photo booth.

'My god,' said Casper. 'Wasn't that the exhibition Chuck and you were at yesterday?'

I nodded. The full significance of the photograph was starting to dawn on me.

'Was anyone hurt?' I managed to ask.

'Doesn't seem so,' said Casper. 'They managed to evacuate the whole place before it went off.'

Casper caught sight of my face.

'Pretty shaking, isn't it, when you have a near miss like that?'

I nodded again speechlessly. In one mind-blowing split-second I'had had a flash of insight. No photo booth . . . no way back . . . no way! . . . oh no! . . . this just couldn't be happening to me.

'How about another cup of tea,' said Casper sympathetically. 'Sometimes a shock like this can be beneficial. Makes you realize how lucky you are to be alive. Best thing to do is forget it – get out and get some nice fresh air.'

I sat nodding like a noddy dog – my mind racing.

How long was I going to be stuck like this for godsake? – marooned in this half-life – no, correction, non-life. I mean, frankly, you could hardly call being male *living* – it was no life, with no flirting, no flaunting, no dressing up in decent designer labels . . . without glossies, girls'-nights-out, gossip-swapping, boy-snogging, SHOPPING! Without even having a choice of ways to do your hair!

Casper broke in through this morbid train of thought.

'So why don't you come down to the allotment with me. I could do with the help actually.'

(Allotment!) That brought a whole new agonizing set of scenarios to mind – ghastly visions of me getting bogged down in all those things males were expected to do, all that mastering of manual skills, and heaving things around. Things like clearing drains and scrambling up ladders and under cars – all that getting wet and sweaty and covered in oil and soil and grot and filth that men are instinctively meant to thrive on . . .

'Here you are, just the job, these should fit.' Casper was passing me a pair of gumboots and a fisherman's smock. A fisherman's smock!

There seemed to be no way out of this. Casper was standing expectantly holding the back door open. I thrust my head through the neck of the smock and pulled it down. Well, at any rate, there was one consolation. In the highly unlikely event that I should happen to bump into anyone I knew at this unearthly hour of a Sunday morning, no one in a million years would dream it was me dressed like this. But then – a doubly depressing thought – they wouldn't anyway, would they, trapped as I was in my present sexual status? – God, this was a mess!

The allotment was on a piece of wasteland that had got stranded between the tube line and the freeway. It must have been a dismal place at the best of times, but today was a particularly damp grey day. Bonfires belched thin smoke half-heartedly into the pollution-saturated air.

I trudged down an uneven muddy path behind Casper feeling like death. He strode ahead making cheery weather-related greetings to the other allotment holders. Eventually, we came to a halt at a patch of earth which was distinguished by a stick marked 'PLOT 242'.

'Well, what do you think?' said Casper.

I stared at the straggling lines of wilting tomatoes and the sagging bean sticks and didn't know what to say.

'Looks like a lot of work,' I ventured.

'Yes, but well worth it. Just think, we're practically self-sufficient in terms of vegetables and all grown in Inner London!'

He dragged something forked and hairy out of the soil and knocked the dirt off it against his boot.

'Just look at that,' he said.

I wondered whether he was expecting congratulations or commiserations. Whatever it was, didn't look a bit like any of the plump clean vegetables wrapped in clingfilm that Mummy brings back from Sainsbury's.

'Right,' said Casper. 'What would you rather do? Turn the compost or tackle some of the weeding?'

It was a difficult decision – but I plumped for the weeding.

He pointed me in the direction of a bed of broccoli seedlings and handed me a trowel and sieve.

I worked pretty hard. I thought it might help the pounding in my head and tight dry feeling in my chest.

Casper was dividing his time between digging and keeping a weather eye on an acrid-smelling bonfire and left me to it.

I was a bit doubtful about some of the weeds but, in spite of it being very small and underdeveloped, I reckoned I could recognize broccoli when I saw it.

After half an hour or so, Casper came over and leaned on a spade for a breather.

Suddenly his expression changed.

'Where's the broccoli gone?' he asked.

I pointed it out to him.

'I suppose . . .' said Casper some time later, when he had dug out all the groundsel and replanted the broccoli, 'I suppose you don't have the same kind of weeds in Mauritius.'

By that time I was turning compost anyway and was past speech. I was lifting tentative forkfuls from the surface trying not to look too hard at the stuff I was unearthing. Every forkful was positively oozing decay and riddled with liver-coloured eel-worms.

Casper was leaning on his spade again, watching critically.

'You want to get down inside the pit,' he said. 'You'll get a better purchase on the stuff from there.'

Well, the way I was feeling I couldn't feel much worse, so I did as he advised.

By the end of the morning I reckon I knew what grave-robbing must be like.

Then Casper slapped me on the back with a filth-encrusted gardening glove and suggested a pint.

Five

Eventually, after I had been *rewarded* by a long stand in an icy pub downing a freezing lager, we returned to Chuck's house. Chuck, who had just emerged from bed, was heading for the kitchen in search of Coco Pops.

'Feeling better?' he asked, when he'd had his first spoonful.

'Listen,' I said, closing the kitchen door behind me. 'I'm in deep s★★★, man!'

Chuck raised an enquiring eyebrow.

I thrust the newspaper in front of him.

Chuck read the headline, munching on his cereal and then he munched more slowly . . .

'Oh dear . . .' he said. And then as he read on, 'Oh dear, oh dear, oh dear.' A slow whistle escaped from between his teeth as he looked at the picture.

'What am I going to do?'

'Have a bowl of Coco Pops . . .'

I took his advice. There's nothing like Coco Pops for concentrating the mind.

We munched silently together.

Chuck cleared his throat.

Maybe he'd thought of something . . .?

'Would you pass the Coco Pops, please,' he said.

He poured himself another bowl and went on eating.

'Perhaps, if we went to Olympia . . .' I started.

'The whole place is probably still sealed off,' he said.

'The worst thing is . . . the photo booth . . . you can see it in the picture . . . blown up . . .' I said trying to keep my voice steady. 'And what about that woman . . . Julie.'

'It says there were no casualties.'

'No casualties!' I said. 'What about me!'

'That's a point,' said Chuck. 'At least it explains where you've disappeared to, though. Everyone will think you were blown up.'

'True,' I said and then: 'My god, you're right!'

An intensely moving picture of my family grieving for me leapt to mind. And then, worse! They were trying to decide who to give all my gear to!

'Geesus, what a mess,' I said. 'I'd better call home!'

'What on earth are you going to say?' asked Chuck. 'Anyway. Chill it, man. They think you're at Franz's, remember?'

'Oh, right, sure . . . We'd better ring Franz and tell her I'm staying over another night.'

At least this would give us a breathing space.

Chuck leaned his chair back and reached for the phone.

The phone rang for quite some time and then, 'Hello,' piped a voice at the other end.

It was a young female voice. Fresh, chirpy and with distinct Mansard Hall overtones. But it wasn't Franz.

Chuck overbalanced backwards and fell in a heap on the floor.

'Chryst, it's you,' he gasped, his hand cupped over the mouthpiece.

'It can't be . . .' I whispered.

'Hello . . . Who's there?' the voice continued. 'Who is this?'

'It's me, Chuck.'

'Oh hi . . . I thought you'd got bombed in that beastly exhibition . . .'

'Let me listen . . .' I grabbed the receiver.

(The voice sounded like a cross between Princess Di and Goldie Hawn.)

'That's not me,' I hissed to Chuck.

'Who's that with you?' the voice demanded.

'No one . . . just a friend,' said Chuck, repossessing the phone.

'Oh really? Who?'

'No one you know. Look, I just rang to see if you got to Franz's OK.'

'Why the brotherly concern?'

'Bombs and things – you know. Just wondered, that's all.'

'You want to meet up today? Want to speak to Franz? She's steaming herself in the sauna.'

'Look, no. Not at the moment. Must dash. I'll ring you, OK?'

Chuck rang off and stared up at me from the floor.

'Oh my God,' he said, breathlessly.

'That can't have been me,' I said. 'I don't sound a bit like that.'

'I can assure you. That was you,' said Chuck. 'I should know. How many times have I called you up for godsake?'

'It can't have been. *I'm here*,' I insisted.

'Listen . . . in a way it does make sense . . .' said Chuck, talking fast, 'just think, when you're having a virtual reality experience, I mean, like in that space race, you're just sitting there, experiencing it, aren't you? Although in your mind you're somewhere else. I mean, in a way, it's kind of like you're in two places at once . . .'

'You mean, you're trying to say there are *two of me*?' I cut in.

'Well, yes, if you like. There's the "real" you we just spoke to on the phone and then there's the "alternative" you that's here with me.'

'What you're trying to say,' I said, trying to follow his lightning train of thought, 'is that I am currently two people in two different places?' This was no joke, man. And I didn't much like the implied negative of being called the 'alternative' either.

'I 'spose so. . . . Yes.'

'Boy!' I said. 'This is getting weirder and weirder.'

'Well, one thing is solved anyway.'

'What's that?'

'We won't have to explain anything to your parents.'

'True.'

We went to Olympia anyway. It seemed the only thing to do. We felt drawn there, as they say criminals are drawn back to the scene of their crime. But Chuck was right. The whole place was sealed off.

'Can't anyone tell us when it will be open again?' asked Chuck.

'It won't. Not that exhibition anyway,' said the security guard who had caught us snooping around at the back of the stadium. 'It'll probably be weeks before they've tidied this lot up. Forensic are in there at the moment sifting through the rubble. What a mess!' he added with the barely concealed satisfaction of someone basking in the limelight of a real live disaster.

Chuck and I made our way back to Chiswick feeling most depressed. As the bus headed back west in the opposite direction from Chelsea and 122 Cheyne Walk (otherwise known, in former, happier times, as 'home'), I suffered a really massive wave of homesickness. I could just picture myself back in my natural habitat having a hot bath well laced with Mummy's Eau Sauvage and then getting into my dressing gown. Grampy (my grandmother) had given me this really gross-looking, but divinely soft and warm, woolly dressing gown for Christmas.

'What's up?' said Chuck.

'I was just thinking about my pink fluffy dressing gown,' I said with a sigh.

About six pairs of eyes turned and stared at me. Chuck sank into his seat and tried to look as if he weren't there.

'And my fluffy slippers!' I added defiantly.

Back at the Davis' I decided to give up the battle of maintaining consciousness. My night of sin was catching up with me. The bump on the back of my head was throbbing. My eyeballs were starting to feel as if they'd been lightly poached. I had prickling sensations going up and down my spine and my body, in general, felt as if I had put on someone else's skin by mistake – which, I had in a way, I suppose. I climbed into the top bunk fully dressed and absolutely nothing else registered until the next morning.

Chuck was shaking me.

'I've had an idea!' he said.

'Oh yeah?'

He was waving the 'Virtual Reality Exhibition' catalogue at me.

'It suddenly occurred to me that it lists the names and addresses of all the exhibitors,' he said.

I shot into a sitting position and hit my head hard on the ceiling, so I lay down again.

'Look,' continued Chuck. 'There's an address for "Alternative Reality Inc". Wasn't that what that Julie woman's booth thing was called?'

I nodded and took the catalogue. The address was in a place called Gants Hill and there was a telephone number too.

We had to wait till Maggie went out before we could use the phone in private. She took forever. She was heading off to her 'Assertion Training for Women' class. Frankly, I thought she was quite assertive enough already, but maybe that just proved that the course was working.

Anyway, she was pretty expert at bossing us around. By the time she left we had the low-down on how to sort our washing into whites and coloureds, load the washing machine, unload it, how to hang things on the line, how not to leave the lights on and how to double-lock if we went out.

'Have a nice day,' called out Chuck as a parting shot to Maggie as she left – it was an expression she loathed.

We got on the phone right away, only to be rewarded with the 'unobtainable tone'. Chuck dialled 100.

'The line in question is currently out of service,' we were informed by the operator.

'Yeah, we know that, but for how long? Is it temporary or what? This is important. A . . . a . . . matter of life and death.' Chuck was laying it on.

'I'm sorry, caller. I'm not at liberty to divulge any more information,' replied the operator, as if it was classified info from MI5 or something.

'Geesus,' said Chuck, slamming down the receiver. 'Now we'll have to get ourselves over there. Where did it say?'

We studied the tube map. At length, on a far-distant, outflung branch of the Metropolitan line we spotted the station – Gants Hill.

We prepared rations for the journey.

'Crunchy or smooth,' asked Chuck, as he spread stone-ground wholemeal with peanut butter. I opted for crunchy, I reckoned I was going to need the extra nourishment.

To conserve water (and time), we flung the whites and coloureds in the wash together, then turned the dial to

Economy Wash. So we set out with a totally clear ecological conscience.

Actually, as tube maps go, there are few places further from Chiswick than Gants Hill. On the journey, in order to while away the time, Chuck initiated me into the game of Bonkers.

Bonkers is a game he and the guys had invented for tube travel. It doesn't refer to insanity but the other use of the word. It goes as follows: you each choose a couple in your compartment, and under the cover of a newspaper or magazine, observe them closely. First you lay bets as to whether they actually *do it* together and then you have to prove it. You get points for things like glances and giggles; holding hands, for instance, scores five and a quick snog gets you a ten. Points are knocked off for obvious downers like yawns, scratching and anti-social nose-blowing. Anyway, I thought I was on to a dead-sure bet. I mean, females are so much better at judging these things, aren't they? I'd selected this wildly loose and lovely looking couple who were obviously madly in love and eyeing each other up like crazy across the central aisle.

I had got to a score of fifteen and Chuck hadn't even scored five with a Sloaney pair who were most obviously married – she was even wearing a wedding ring, for goodness sake. Then the male of my couple got up and abruptly left the train without so much as a goodbye or a glance in the girl's direction.

A fierce argument broke out between us.

'See. They didn't even know each other,' hissed Chuck.

'Rubbish, they'd just had this flaming row, that's all.'

We got through six couples by the time we reached Gants Hill and I owed Chuck two quid. So you can tell how far it was.

Surfacing into the cruel light of East London, I was starting to feel a bit tense about what would happen if we did find Julie. I mean, would she simply be able to swop me back just like that or what? And if she did what would it *feel* like? I guess this is what parachutists experience before a jump. It's the kind of tension people call 'character-building'.

Anyway, it took some time to locate the right road. Gants Hill is a lost world pitted by roundabouts and criss-crossed by link roads. By the look of it, a territory rich in opportunity for double-glazing salesmen and home improvement specialists. Beyond a parade of shops with names like Do-ya-mow, Gnomeville and Grecian Ernie's, we located the street we were looking for: Colchester Drive. The houses which must have once been identical rows of 'thirties semis had been lovingly customized with no expense spared.

'Look, that one's got its front path up its front wall,' said Chuck pointing out a particularly lively one covered in crazy paving.

Decorative nets twitched behind latticed windows as we searched in vain for Number 289.

And then we found what we were looking for. Or at least we didn't. Set between two particularly acute victims of 'Gants Hill syndrome' – Number 287 which was adorned with an impressive row of Corinthian columns, and Number 291 which was in red brick painstakingly repointed with turquoise cement – was what looked like a demolition site. The windows were all boarded up and there was an irregular fence of up-ended doors all across the front.

Chuck heaved a rusting piece of corrugated iron aside and we made our way up the front path. A small plaque swinging on a single screw to the right of the door was inscribed with the words, 'Alternative Reality Inc'.

'We've come to the right place,' said Chuck.

There wasn't a bell so we banged on the door and peered through the letterbox.

Inside there was a vast pile of dusty mail and a piece of flex attached to a box marked 'BT'.

'I can see why we had difficulty getting through,' I said.

The next door neighbour behaved in the way that next door neighbours do when they're interviewed about serial killers and people.

'No, they were very quiet. Kept themselves to themselves. . . .'

Then she mumbled something about blokes in bowler hats who came and took all the furniture away.

'Bailiffs!' she said with a knowing look.

Chuck and I exchanged glances.

'Well that's a bit of a bummer,' said Chuck as we made our way despondently back to the tube station.

'A *bit of a bummer*! Is that all you can say?'

'What do you expect me to say?'

'Look, until we find that woman I'm going to have to stay this way. I mean, GOD! Imagine how I feel. Stuck like this . . . I mean, it's simply totally unspeakably *gross* . . . how can you *stand* it, being male? . . . Yukkk!'

Chuck looked rather offended. 'It's not as bad as all that,' he said.

'Oh for godsake, Chuck, think of something!'

'I can't.'

We sat on the tube in silence.

The truly seriously ghastly nature of the situation was starting to get to me in a big way. What if we *never* found Julie? Basically it meant I could never get back to my normal *female* self again. Suddenly, I saw the total bleakness of the future stretching out before me . . . NIGHTMARE! Nothing but a whole featureless time-span of maleness to look forward to . . . All that having to pretend to be macho and masterful. All that one-upmanship and in-talk about cars and sport and stuff. All that being-one-of-the-boys and having to down oceans of lukewarm bitter standing up and pretending to like it!

And then I thought further forward to all that long-term stuff about being expected to 'make a living' and 'support people' – I mean, how can it be called a 'living' endlessly grinding along as a poor underprivileged male? . . . expected to trudge your way up a steady promotional ladder . . . nine to five till sixty-five. Sixty-five! I mean males don't even live as long as we do – No wonder! The poor sods . . .

'Well, I guess you'd better stay on at my place, for the time being at any rate,' said Chuck.

I nodded miserably.

Where I lived was the least of my problems. I was trying to come to terms with this devastating new vision of *the rest of my life*.

Several aeons later, back at Chuck's house, we found Maggie fuming over the washing. I mean personally, I couldn't see what all the fuss was about. We were the ones who were going to have to wear the tie-dyed shocking-pink Y-fronts.

'And,' said Maggie, slamming the bag of pegs down on the kitchen table, 'I suggest you start getting your things ready for tomorrow.'

'Tomorrow?' said Chuck blankly.

'Yes, term starts tomorrow, remember?'

'But I don't go back till the 30th,' said Chuck.

'Tomorrow *is* the 30th,' said Maggie. And then she started sounding off about how absolutely useless Chuck was at organizing his life.

So I decided tactfully to make myself scarce and headed for the bedroom.

I was just reaching the half landing when I heard Maggie's voice through the crack in the kitchen doorway.

' . . . and how long is he meant to be staying, anyway . . .?'

I paused.

'Well it's hard to say . . .' I could hear Chuck stalling her.

'Where's his luggage then? I'm sick of him wearing your clothes.'

'Lost,' I heard Chuck say. 'In flight . . . yeah, he's trying to. He keeps calling the airline.'

Then a piercing whisper. 'So, what's he going to be doing all day?'

'No worries, he'll be at school with me. He's joining the Sixth at North Thames.'

I nearly fell backwards down the stairs. Me . . . at North Thames . . . a Comprehensive! (Otherwise crudely known as the Gas Board, by the girls of Mansard Hall.) Culture shock!

When Chuck came into the bedroom, I was waiting for him.

'You don't expect me to go to your school, do you? I mean, Geesus, I don't even speak the language.'

Chuck shrugged. 'Well, you can't hang around here all day. Maggie'd go spare. So it seemed like the best idea.'

'Won't they wonder what I'm doing there? I mean, people have to enrol or something, don't they?' (It had recently occurred to me that the one compensation of not being the real me was being able to skip school and veg out all day in front of videos.)

'No worries,' said Chuck. 'The Sixth Form bit is separate, different teachers and everything. You'll just have to make sure none of them think you're studying their subject.'

'So what am I going to do all day?' I asked.

'Just chill out in the Common Room. Or in the Library, everyone will think you've got "frees". You could even get some work done.'

'*Great* . . .' I said.

The prospect of the next day was really depressing. So I crept down to the sitting room to get stuck into my daily supply of *Neighbours* and *Home and Away* in order to cheer myself up.

The theme music had just started and I was making myself really comfortable on the sofa when Maggie came in.

'I didn't know boys watched *Neighbours*,' she said.

'I don't see why not,' I said.

'All those "heartfelt relationships" – I mean, it's women's stuff, isn't it?' she said.

Honestly, this was sexism of the very worst kind. And from Maggie, too.

I decided to ignore her comments and to watch them all the same. Maggie kind of hovered. Frankly, I think she was into secret *Neighbours* abuse – she was obviously dying to put her feet up and home in, but she wasn't going to come clean and admit she was addicted.

After *Neighbours* there was a really weepy episode of *Home and Away*. I mean, I had to get out Chuck's handkerchief and blow my nose three times.

When it ended I had this massive lump in my throat and I decided to head for the bathroom in case I started howling in a most unmanly manner.

I had to skirt round Chuck who was sorting through grass-stained sportswear on the landing. When he asked me what was up, I pretended to have a coughing fit.

I mean males don't cry, do they?

Six

So . . . that's why we were standing by the bus stop at the unearthly hour of 7.45 am next day. I mean, I'm really sensitive to time changes. The sudden switch from a decent lunchtime awakening to attending the dawn chorus and I suffer from serious jet-lag.

Chuck didn't look too hot either.

In actual fact, as it turned out, school wasn't such a brilliant idea of Chuck's anyway.

The day kicked off with the typical start-of-year pep talk from the North Thames Head. There were so many Sixth Formers, I mean like two hundred of them, both boys and girls, crowded into this Assembly Hall. After the Head had finished telling us what we all already knew, i.e. how we were about to embark on the two most crucial years of our lives (but maybe he was referring to our academic lives not our sex-lives), this Health Freak took over and started talking about educating the whole person – body and mind. The importance of sport to kind of clear the brain etc. so that you could work better. I was taking this all in like mad until I realized the implications.

Before I knew quite what was happening, this hangover from the Nazi Youth Movement had separated the boys from the girls. Chuck luckily had restrained me as I was heading off to the wrong side of the Hall. The girls were trotted off for some nice warm indoor aerobics and civilized games of netball. And the boys were herded down into these really gross, freezing cold changing rooms that smelt of decomposing gym shoes.

Chuck found some abandoned seventeenth-hand gym shorts for me and everyone started stripping off. Actually, it was just as well it was me who was going through all this and not Franz. I mean, for sixteen or so, some of those boys were really well-developed! Naturally, I did my best to keep my eyes decently averted but boys just don't have the same sense of modesty as girls.

I manoeuvred my way into a fairly private corner of the room, and tried to get changed as inconspicuously as possible.

But the minute I unbuttoned my Levi's, a bedlam of whistles and cat-calls were unleashed. You just wouldn't believe the novelty-value of shocking-pink Y-fronts.

I was saved from all this 'flattering' attention by the room in general turning to an even greater attraction. The changing room door was flung open and who should stride in but . . . *Alex*.

His entrance was greeted by a chorus of 'Hey Alex, you missed the indoctrination.' 'Where you been, man?' 'What you been up to?'

Alex cast a glance over the admiring crowd and waited for a lull.

'Bimbo-shagging,' he said, with a broad grin and slid his T-shirt over his head revealing a perfectly bronzed torso.

I hitched the shorts up, brushed the hair back out of my eyes, tried to look less of a wally, kind of automatically checking myself out in the nearest mirror. Oh boy! It's amazing how easy it is to forget little things like what gender you are!

'Hey, you been knocking off that Francesca tart?' shouted a boy from across the room.

I pricked up my ears. There was a crude chorus of whistles.

'Nah, she was with me last night,' shouted another boy. 'My turn had come around again.'

Alex picked up a damp towel from a pile on the floor and flicked it at the offending boy. At that point a fairly general sort of fight broke out and I was just about to resort to climbing on top of the lockers when Fritz or Helmut, or whatever this Youth Leader was called, appeared with a whistle and called us to order. Suddenly, we were all filing out like prisoners of war into the freezing drizzle. Then, before I could object, I found I had been picked for a soccer team.

I'm not sure to this day if the rules for soccer bear any resemblance to those of netball. But (using feet in place of hands) I stuck to them all the same. When I wasn't lying flat in the mud, I was being kicked and whistled at and given offside – wherever that might be – and generally jeered at by everyone. In the end I found the best policy was to get tripped up as much as possible and then the other team seemed to get whistled at more.

During one of these bouts on the ground I became conscious of a lot of shouting and cheering coming from the next door pitch. A group of girls who had escaped from the netball team were standing on the sidelines looking on with a kind of breathless concentration. They suddenly broke into a chorus of screams.

The cause of all this admiration came steaming up the field. *Alex* had just taken and scored a free kick and now was showing off like mad, running round in order to get hugged. I watched with reluctant admiration as this perfect piece of male machinery went pounding down the sidelines. There wasn't so much as a dab of mud on those golden-brown hairy legs.

Meanwhile, I was being whistled at like mad and I was dragged back into the thick of it. I wasn't really conscious of anything but feet, flying mud, and trying to avoid the ball until, about ten minutes after half time, out of the corner of my eye I caught sight of a small group of people on the next door pitch gathered round a figure lying on the ground. That's when the ball came flying towards me and I instinctively headed it, more in self-defence than anything else.

It was difficult to see what was happening because of everyone gathering round to congratulate me. It was the only goal either side had scored on our pitch. But I managed to get a glimpse of a body being carried off on a stretcher, and when the teams started playing again neither Alex nor his supporters were anywhere to be seen.

Later, back in the changing rooms, Chuck had saved me a shower next to his.

'What happened to Alex?'

'Ripped a tendon,' said Chuck. 'I told him he'd been training too hard. You OK?'

'Just counting my bruises.'

'What's the final score?'

'Eleven.'

Chuck sympathetically passed his Wash and Go over the partition.

'Perhaps you'd better try and duck out of games next time,' he suggested.

I sloshed shampoo over my head, thinking of Alex prone like that and wondering if those girls were still with him – the tarts. I hadn't got a really good look at them but I could picture the taller one (and, depressingly enough, she had quite a decent body actually) holding a limp paw maybe or mopping sweat off his perfectly formed brow – some girls get all the luck.

After that Chuck had an A-level Physics period, so I headed off to the Library. The North Thames Library was vast compared with Mansard Hall's. Mansard Hall's smelt of apple cores and nail varnish, it was a good place to settle in for an intimate chat or even a doze, well concealed between shelves of decently out-of-date leather-bound books. North Thames's was packed with ferociously new-looking paperbacks. The metal shelving was labelled numerically and alphabetically and set out in clinical rows between acres of shiny wood-grain-effect formica tables. An icy light came in through picture windows which overlooked the grim rutted mud of the playing fields. God, it was bleak.

I was the only person in there, apart from the Librarian, who when I entered started trying to look busy shuffling her index cards. Every footstep I made resounded on the highly polished parquet. I clopped down to the far end of the room and managed to find a seat which was partially obscured from the Librarian's view.

I must have been sitting there gazing into space for some minutes – my mind still deeply engrossed on the subject of *Alex* – when the Librarian, obviously overcome by curiosity, came down to my end of the room with a pile of books. She put them down on a table and our eyes met.

'Can I help at all?' she said.

'No I'm fine actually. Thanks all the same,' I said.

She turned and huffily started to thrust books on to the shelves.

When she had finished, she swung round and gave me another long hard look and then trotted back to her desk. I watched her back, lumpy and resolutely bra-less under her acrylic cardie. She was the kind of woman who made you want to creep up behind her and shout 'Madonna' very loudly in her ear.

But, after all, this was a library. It was quite possible that she was merely expecting me to take an interest in her books.

Dutifully, I got to my feet and started to nose my way along the shelves. My boots went clop, clop, clop, as I worked my way through the Physical Sciences and Applied Molecular Biology sections.

The Sciences led on to Social Sciences. In it, there was an entire bookcase labelled 'Women's Interests'. It held title after title of things like *Women's Place in a Male Dominated World, The Second Sex, Social Aspects of Gender,* etc. etc. I slipped a book out. Basically, it was all pretty predictable stuff about the sex war, but all written in very long and complicated language with everything spelt the American way like 'dialog' and 'behavior'. It occurred to me that if there were all these books about 'Women's Interests' there must be some on 'Men's' and currently it wouldn't do me any harm to swot up a bit on the 'Un-Fair Sex', since it seemed to be the one I was currently stuck with.

I was just taking the umpteenth book out, and had built up quite a pile on the side, searching for some tiny snippet of info on the male of the species, when I came face to face with the Librarian who was working her way down the other side and had ended up bang opposite me, glaring through a gap between the books.

She was square-faced by nature and wore her hair firmly anchored across her forehead with a kirby grip. She certainly didn't do herself any favours when she was looking cross.

'Are you trying to find something in particular?' she asked, directing a piercing glance at my pile of books.

Clearly she thought I was trespassing on female territory.

'Yes,' I said, 'as a matter of fact I am. Have you got anything on "Men's Interests"?'

She drew herself up to her full height and swept around to my side of the shelf. After a lot of searching index pages and slamming books in and out she came up with a single slim volume.

Men's Studies, it was called.

I accepted it with due expressions of gratitude and sidled

back to my seat. It turned out to be a load of essays by feminist writers anyway.

Chuck came to find me at lunchtime.

'Had a good morning?' he asked once we had fought our way through the lunch queue and secured two plates of shepherd's pie and chips.

I struggled with my mouthful to reply. Boy, I certainly had found out what it was like to be hungry. I guess it probably had something to do with having about 700 million additional cells to keep alive. Every one of them was screaming out for nourishment.

'I'd rather not talk about it,' I said, shovelling in another mouthful.

'What you doing this afternoon? Going back to the Library?'

I shook my head.

'I think I'll risk the Common Room. Do you think the guys have got over their colour prejudice yet?'

Chuck frowned. They'd been giving him a hard time about the pink Y-fronts as well.

'Guess you're going to have to brave it some day,' he said.

So I went to the Common Room.

As it happened, it was empty. I shifted a load of magazines off a rotting armchair and settled down for a snooze.

Could I get some peace? No such luck. There was a knock at the door and a head shot round it.

'Hi! I'm Jenny Pearson,' she said. 'Just checking . . . and you seem to be the only lost sheep from my fold.'

'Sorry?' I said.

'You Arts or Sciences?' she demanded.

'Arts,' I said. 'But I've got a "free" . . .'

'Uh . . . uh . . .' she said. 'No one has a "free" first pm period Tuesday. It's General Studies. You ought to take a look at your timetable occasionally you know.'

Before I could object, I found I was being herded down

69

the corridor to a classroom filled to bursting point with a very noisy combination of males and females.

A whistle went round.

'Here comes Day-glo,' someone whispered.

'Give us a flash,' whooped another voice. And the whole class fell about.

Ms Pearson pretended she hadn't heard this.

'What did you say your name was?' she asked me.

'I didn't. It's Jake.'

'OK Jake, you sit down right here and then we can get started.'

After Ms had given us a long piece of propaganda on the vital nature of knowing very little about an awful lot – i.e. General Studies – we got down to business. And the business that Tuesday was showing us how absolutely rivetingly relevant Shakespeare currently was to simply everybody's lives.

' . . . the timeless nature of his humour, for instance . . .' Ms was getting into full flow. I was just dozing off when I heard her say, 'So who's going to volunteer to be our readers. We need one boy and one girl, please.'

There was a dead silence broken only by the shuffling of feet.

'Right,' said Ms. 'In that case I'll choose. How about you, Jake, since you're so keen to be involved in everything. Would you mind standing up?'

She handed me a Penguin version of *Twelfth Night*.

'I'll read the girl, Miss,' a girl along the front row, three down from me, who had bright red lipsticky lips, leaped to her feet.

'Good,' said Ms. She went on to explain the basics of the play.

'The thing to remember,' she said, 'is that in Shakespeare's day girls were usually played by boys. They'd be dressed in women's clothes and wearing wigs of course. But this didn't fool the audience, they would have been only too aware that the "lovely" heroine they were watching was a boy dressed up. Now, Class, what you have to remember is that Jake is actually a girl, disguised as a boy . . .'

I nearly dropped my book – was the woman clairvoyant or something . . .?

' . . . so basically what you're watching is a boy, playing a girl – Viola, but she's disguised herself as a boy, calling herself Cesario. He (or rather she) is being chatted up by a girl – Olivia, who of course, would also be played by a boy. All quite simple really when you work it out . . . OK, Jake . . . you're Viola, from the top of page 191 please.'

My mind was doing double back-flips.

Here was I, a boy who was actually a girl, reading the part of a boy acting the part of a girl, disguised as a boy . . . oh boy!

'Come on, Jake, we're all waiting.'

'Sorry. . . . "Grace and good disposition tend you ladyship" . . . errm. . . . "You'll nothing madam to your Lord by me?" ' . . . I stammered out in a sort of monotone.

Lush-lips fluttered her eyelashes at me.

' "Stay," ' . . . she sighed. ' "I pr'ythee tell me what thou thinkst of me?" '

Her performance was greeted by appreciative whoops and wolf-whistles from the class.

We continued despite the clamour:

(Me): ' "That you do think you are not what you are." '

(Lush-lips): ' "If I think so, I think the same of you." '

(Me): ' "Then think you right I am not what I am." '

Someone hissed 'Day-glo drawers' and the class collapsed into a convulsive group-snigger.

Lush-lips: ' "Oh I would you were as I would have you be!" '

She left out nothing in the saying of this line.

I felt myself go scarlet right down to approximately my navel.

Ms held up her hand and waited until the general uproar had subsided.

'Well,' she said with satisfaction. 'I think we've proved one thing. The way you reacted was just as an audience of the time would have done. Audience participation was much more common in Shakespeare's day. What you were reacting to, in such a lively manner, is called "dramatic irony" . . .'

Ms rabbited on for a while about what irony meant . . . little did she know the true irony of the situation.

After General Studies everyone was let off early since it was the first day of term. I found Chuck lingering near the front gates waiting for me. He was making calculations on his scientific calculator but he shoved it in his pocket when he caught sight of me.

'What were you doing?'

'Just working things out. Had a better afternoon?'

'I'm not sure if I'm going to fit in here,' I said.

'Really?' said Chuck. 'Why not?'

'I'd rather not say.'

He got it out of me in the end anyway.

'Honestly, I've been called much worse things than Dayglo drawers,' said Chuck.

'I just feel so humiliated,' I said. 'Incidentally, isn't that our bus?' I had caught sight of a Number 191 heading towards us.

'I thought we might walk back,' said Chuck. 'It's not very far.'

'Walk back! Geesus, after all that soccer . . .!'

Then I caught sight of his face.

'It's money, isn't it? I've been sponging off you . . . God, I feel awful.'

'It's only that I'm not sure if we can hold out till the end of the month – you know: double lunches, your fares, that taxi. Our finances are finite, you know.'

'God, I just didn't think . . .' I said.

Actually, we didn't get round to talking about money

just then because at that point something happened which temporarily erased everything from my mind.

'Hi,' shouted a familiar voice.

I caught sight of Henry. (Short for Henrietta, one of my best buddies from Mansard Hall.) She was standing at the school gates waving frantically.

But my eyes were on the person who was with her.

There was no mistaking her.

It was *ME*!

Seven

Can you imagine what it's like to actually come face to face with *yourself*? Honestly, it *totally freaked me out*. I hadn't felt this shy since I chatted up Rob Lowe in the Shuckbrugh pub (until I realized he was only someone who looked like him).

'No man, really, I can't face this,' I whispered to Chuck.

'Come on,' said Chuck. 'Better get it over with.'

Chuck sauntered up to the school gates and I tailed along trying to stay kind of shielded behind him.

'Hi!' said Henry and gave him a smacker on both cheeks.

'Hi Justine,' said Chuck, and this vision of *me* leaned over and permitted itself to be kissed.

'Who's your friend?' asked Henry.

'Oh this is Jake . . . he's new . . . to North Thames, I mean . . . starting this term,' said Chuck.

'Hi there!' said Henry.

And *'Justine'* said nothing but *our eyes met*.

My stomach did a double-somersault as I thought that she MUST recognize me! I mean, I'd faced *her* face a million times in the mirror. It was *so-oo* familiar! Although, of course, I wasn't looking at it in reverse this time as I was used to. In fact, I'd never noticed before but surely I had one eyebrow slightly higher than the other? Come to think of it, it was about time I plucked my eyebrows . . .

She (meaning me) stared at me fixedly for a few seconds and just the shadow of a frown passed across her face. Then she turned and looked in the opposite direction, where absolutely nothing was happening.

The way she so blatantly ignored my gaze actually made me feel worse.

(Just imagine what it's like not being recognized by someone you know *that well* – I mean actually being introduced to them like a total stranger – and then, on top of it all, having to refer to yourself in *the third person*! I mean, seriously, talk about an identity crisis!)

I think I must have been staring at her a bit too long or something, because, after a few moments, she seemed really embarrassed. She kept flicking her hair back and letting it flop down again. For some reason, she was getting really hot and bothered.

I guess Chuck noticed because he cleared his throat loudly and said: 'So how's things? Did you just happen to be passing or couldn't you live without me?'

'Mansard doesn't start till next week so we had time to kill,' said Justine. (That's true! My term didn't start for yonks! Geesus, I should be on holiday, man!)

'We came to pick up Alex, actually,' said Henry. 'Or at least *Justine* did.'

Chuck explained how Alex had been 'picked up' already.

'Really?!' said Henry and demanded a full account of the gruesome details – she was the scientist of Mansard Hall and had ambitions to go into Pathology or Taxidermy or something – 'Where is he now? Hadn't we better go and check out whether he's still alive or not?'

'Someone said they took him into Charing Cross,' said Chuck.

At the mention of the Hospital, Henry demanded that we should all go and visit him there. It was on the way home after all. She started herding us down the road towards Hammersmith Broadway.

When the pavement narrowed, Henry grabbed Chuck's arm and whispered something in his ear. Justine and I were kind of forced to tag along behind them, walking side by side.

I racked my brains for some way in which, without making a total wally of myself, I could establish whether or not she had any idea of *who I really was*.

We passed three bus stops before I came to the decision that there was *no way* I could even *begin* to think of a cool and laid-back way of finding out.

It was Justine who broke the silence in the end.

'You know, I've got the weirdest feeling that I've seen you somewhere before.'

Henry, who must have been eavesdropping, swung round at that point and said, 'Geesus Justine! What a corny line! Surely you can do better than that!'

'Shut up, Henry,' said Justine. 'This is a private conversation.'

She turned back to me.

'Where could it have been?' she persisted.

This was a tricky one. Maybe this was the point at which I should have come clean and come out with the whole story. But when it came to the point – words totally failed me. I sent an agonized glance of appeal to Chuck.

'You couldn't have done. He's only just arrived. From Mauritius,' he said.

'Oh really?' she said. 'How long are you here for?' As if that totally settled the matter.

I muttered something about not being sure and gave her another long, hard look.

But she didn't react. She was getting all hot and fiddling with her hair again – most probably due to the fact that we were drawing near to the Hospital and we were about to see *Alex*.

We started our tour of Charing Cross Hospital in Casualty. Henry kept on pointing out really gruesome pieces of equipment and talking about the episodes of *Casualty* she'd watched on TV. Both Justine and I tried to look the other way. I mean, I know I'm a total physical coward and I now discovered that being male didn't help at all (actually, I hardly like to admit this but, in fact, it made things worse).

The female at the 'Enquiries Desk' told us to sit down and wait while she tried to locate Alex.

'God, I hate hospitals,' I said. 'I had to sit in Casualty practically all night once when I broke my little finger.'

Justine stared at me wide-eyed.

'God,' she said. 'That's really w-e-i-r-d! So did I! That's freaky! Which one did you break?'

Chuck gave me a warning frown.

Oh my god! This was such a mess! I was going to have to watch every word I said to her.

Luckily, at that point Henry spotted an ambulance coming in full pelt with its lights flashing.

It turned out only to contain two ambulancemen. I think they were late for their teabreak or something. Anyway, much to Henry's disappointment, they didn't seem to be wheeling in any victims of mass carnage. In fact, the only high spot of our half-hour wait was the accidental entrance of a man who was rather drunk followed by the arrival of a woman who thought she might have sprained her ankle.

The Enquiries Desk Lady, having checked through all her files, eventually announced that Alex had been 'admitted' and directed us to the seventh floor.

We traced our way through corridors smelling of really gross sickly sweet disinfectant to a ward called Male Surgical.

There, propped up on snow-white pillows and spotlit by a shaft of declining sunlight, lay Alex.

He was wearing a pair of borrowed Charing Cross pyjamas casually left unbuttoned to the waist and had a young and rather inexperienced-looking nurse seated beside him taking his pulse.

His eyes were closed and he had a thermometer protruding from a broad grin of satisfaction.

As we approached the bed the nurse whipped the thermometer out of his mouth and studied it.

'Will I live?' moaned Alex.

'Probably,' she said. 'Unless you fall out of bed or something.'

We drew nearer. The nurse shooed us back.

'Only two visitors at a time, please.'

So we had to take it in shifts.

We let the girls go first and waited in the Day Room which had a kind of indoor window overlooking the ward.

Chuck soon got involved in a vast and very complex puzzle of the *Laughing Cavalier* that had been left set out on the coffee table.

I stood at the window in order to monitor the girls' behaviour. I was anxious to check out what Justine was up to. (I know I tend to lose my cool completely if I really fancy someone and the most cringeworthy things kind of slip out just at the very worst moment.)

The girls were leaning over the bed, and kind of drinking in his every word. What I could see of Alex's well-bronzed body was looking delectably helpless.

'What are they doing now?' asked Chuck.

I reported back as much as I could see.

'Henry is checking through his temperature chart and Justine looks as if she's about to suck his big toe.'

'Geesus,' said Chuck. 'Some guys get all the luck.'

'Can't really call it luck, being strapped down in a hospital bed,' I pointed out.

"Spose not. Still he doesn't look too unhappy about it,' he said. He paused and sucked his breath through his teeth. 'He's in better nick than this fellow at any rate.'

'Why, what's wrong with him?'

Chuck was scanning through the pieces at the side.

'Careless sods. Looks like they've gone and lost his left ear.'

A couple of stray visitors who happened to be passing the Day Room paused just long enough to catch the gist of this comment.

They skittered off down the corridor.

'It's the cut-backs you know,' I heard one say.

The other muttered something about 'spare-part surgery'.

'It's all very well if you can afford to go Private . . .'

Anyway, at that point, the girls appeared in the doorway.

'They're probably going to have to operate . . .' said Henry with evident relish.

'He's being so brave,' sighed Justine.

'It's only a torn ligament for godsake, it isn't terminal,' said Chuck – most unsympathetically I thought.

'He's probably stoned up to the eyeballs on hospital issue and loving every minute of it,' he added, as we swopped over as Official Visitors.

Anyway Chuck was right. Alex was in pretty good spirits.

'Hi, fans,' he said. 'Cm'on, where are the grapes and the girlie magazines? I thought you'd come to cheer me up.'

'You look pretty cheered up already,' said Chuck. 'Incidentally, you don't know Jake. . . .' he thrust me forward.

'Only by reputation,' said Alex with a smirk. He waved a hand at me as if he expected me to bow down on one knee and kiss it or something.

'How you feeling?' I asked with devastating originality.

'Horny as hell,' said Alex, raising an eyebrow and licking his lips. 'It's all the attention you get from the talent,' he continued. 'Seeing the male body prone like this really brings out the animal in them.'

'Thought you'd be pleased we brought them along,' said Chuck.

'Not the bimbettes, do me a favour,' said Alex. 'I mean women. Geesus, all that starched white. It really turns me on.'

I didn't believe I was hearing this! All the up-chatting that Alex had indulged in with us – and he had the cheek to call us 'bimbettes'.

'*Bimbettes*!', referring to worldly-wise Henry and so-oo sophisticated me! Geesus, given the opportunity, I was going to have to prove to this young man just what kind of a woman he was referring to in such a dismissive manner.

'Did you see the neat little number checking my vital statistics when you came in?' Alex continued.

'You mean the nurse taking your temperature?' asked Chuck.

'Boy, she was practically climbing into the bed,' said Alex, adjusting his pyjamas so that even more tanned torso was visible.

'Going to find it a bit difficult getting "a leg-over" in your present condition, aren't you?' observed Chuck, gazing at the contraption which was maintaining Alex's right leg at a constant angle of forty-five degrees.

This was the cue for Alex to go into a detailed and very crude description of how to get around the problem. Meanwhile, I indulged in a little heart-searching.

I was coming to a profound and very distressing conclusion about boys of my own age. It went like this:

Up to the age of about twelve, most boys ignore you completely. Then from twelve to about fourteen they idolize your elder sisters (or any female who is round about fully formed and younger than their mother). From fourteen to seventeen there is that indeterminate age when they're not sure if they wouldn't rather idolize each other. And then, just as they're emerging from all this – at the ripe old age of eighteen or so – they start going for younger girls. The depressing conclusion was that boys of one's own age neatly by-pass you at every stage of the process.

Meanwhile Chuck and Alex were still heavily into the technicalities of hospital bed sex. I was starting to wonder precisely how any female could ever achieve a meaningful relationship with Alex. Here was quite some challenge. I mean, basically, Alex didn't need a girlfriend, he got enough sexual thrills from looking at himself in the mirror. It was the kind of male arrogance I'd always found *totally irresistible* . . .

As Chuck and Alex reached hospital bed position number twenty-five, I noticed a knocking on the internal window and found Henry and Justine were waving at us. It seemed they had to be off and with a lot of kiss-blowing and mouthed promises to return, Justine left a massive lipstick kiss on the glass, and gave us one long, last, thoughtful glance. Then she turned, flicked her hair out of her eyes and followed Henry.

We stayed on for ten minutes or so and then a lady in a green nylon overall appeared with a trolley bearing what looked very much like leftovers from North Thames school dinners which, come to think of it, happened to be conveniently just down the road from the Hospital.

'How long do you think you'll be in here?' I asked Alex.

'Long as possible,' said Alex with a wink directed towards the Staff Nurse's room.

And so we left.

'Hardcore mags and something soft and yummy to nibble on next time . . . don't forget now,' Alex called after us.

'Is Alex always like that when you're "all-boys-together"?' I asked Chuck as we made our way back to Chiswick.

'Like what?' asked Chuck.

'Sexually obsessed?'

'Oh yeah,' said Chuck. 'We all are.'

We walked along for a while in silence. I mean it's tragic really – as girls we waste all that energy lusting after blokes, and they're doing the same over us. There's oceans of unexpended passion on both sides of the sexual gulf and none of us ever seem to manage to get it together.

Back in Chiswick we shot through the front door to find the phone ringing.

Maggie had answered it and was standing with her hand held over the receiver.

'Friends of yours,' she said to Chuck with a rare note of disapproval in her voice.

Chuck took the receiver . . .

'Hi there . . .'

Then his language abruptly switched to rave-mode . . .

'Yeah, right. Pukka now. Non muchas to you brain-dead Neanderthals.'

I couldn't quite catch what was said on the other end but the gist of it must have been a demand for further information.

'Blabbed a lot but a good stack and came up glossy again.'

I didn't need to be told who he was talking to – or who he was talking about for that matter.

'Look got to rise a deck. Rental in occupation. OK?'

He put the receiver down and shot up the stairs.

'Hey, slot the lobster,' he shouted down. 'I mean, Jake! Hang up, down there, would you?'

I hung up.

I sat on the stairs, despondently thinking of what a wally I had made of myself on Saturday night. Little fragments of Chuck's conversation penetrated the gloom of the stairwell.

'Went all bitmapp, glitching all over the place . . .'

'......'

'Nah. Bit slack on the plus . . . so no go . . .'

'.....'

'Chill it . . . just clipboard, till I'm "Positive" again. OK?'

I heard the receiver being replaced and Chuck came down the stairs two at a time.

'It's money, isn't it?' I said.

'Don't worry about it,' said Chuck.

'Worry about what?' asked Maggie appearing from the kitchen with a well-greased monkey wrench in her hand.

'I hope you haven't you been listening in,' said Chuck, gazing at the monkey wrench with a frown.

'Gave that up long ago, no point,' said Maggie. 'Anyway, I'm glad you haven't the cash to waste time with that lot. They're a dead loss. Now come and give me a hand with this.'

Maggie had the partially dismembered body of the lawn-mower spread over the kitchen table.

'Isn't that a man's job?' I ventured.

Maggie looked really offended.

She handed me the monkey wrench.

'You tell me,' she said.

Eight

The next day Chuck and I got up at crack of dawn and he prepared for school as usual. Actually, we were both pretty exhausted, we'd been up till 2.00 am struggling with the lawnmower. We had just finished when we found three bits under the kitchen table that had kind of been overlooked. So we put them in the dresser drawer where Maggie keeps her screwdrivers and soldering iron and tenon-joint-cutter and things.

I hadn't slept very well. I had been doing a lot of thinking during the night. And I had made a couple of pretty fundamental decisions. The first was that, even if it meant enlisting MI5, the CIA and the brains of the entire Metropolitan Police Force, I had to find some way of tracking down Julie. The second was that, in the meantime, I had to find some sort of financial support that wouldn't mean sponging off Chuck.

So when Chuck and I got to the bus stop, I turned and said: 'Guess this is where we say goodbye. I'm going the other way.'

'Aren't you coming to school?'

I shook my head. 'I've got to try and find a way of getting my hands on some dosh.'

'Come on. We can get by.'

But I was adamant, and Chuck eventually stepped down. 'Well. Don't turn to crime!' he said.

We stood at opposite sides of the road waiting for our respectively bound buses. Chuck's came first. It was already seething with North Thames lifeform.

As it drove off I was left standing on the other side of the road, a lone figure bound for an uncertain future. As a matter of fact, I felt pretty desolate.

I checked my pockets. Chuck had insisted on giving me all that was left of his money. Our joint fortune stood at precisely four pounds and nine pence in the world. I took the bus to Chelsea Library. Somehow it seemed a suitable midway point between my two lives. Besides, it was warm and it was free.

I found myself a seat between two antique Chelsea ladies and started to search through a copy of the previous day's *Evening Standard* for the jobs page.

The 'Appointments' column mainly consisted of ads for Driver/Owners, Motorcycle Couriers and Secretaries with 50wpm, I was pretty low on wpms and since I didn't own a car or bike, none of this applied to me. I considered other more intriguing titles such as 'Lead Closers' and 'Progress Chasers', both of which sounded terribly frustrating. There were several ads for 'Hoffman Pressers' – but one never knew how tricky Hoffmen were to press.

In fact, nothing quite leapt off the page at me until I came to the specific section entitled 'General Appointments'. Here, it seemed there were massive opportunities for people with my kind of talents and qualifications.

'HELLO', read one ad. 'We are looking for a number of people who can respond to a friendly atmosphere' – that sounded like me. And another: 'HUNGRY FOR MONEY? Make £500–1,000 per week' – that sounded even more like me! I shot out to the phone booth, there was no time to be lost.

After the third phone call, I discovered that I had a lot to learn about small ads: there were technical terms like 'unpressurized training', which basically came down to working for nothing for several weeks on the offchance that they might keep you on afterwards. And there was a big demand for things like CVs, Previous Experience and References. One company even had the cheek to ask me to provide ID although I'm sure my voice sounded as if I was well over eighteen.

By twelve o'clock my stomach was crying out for nourishment and my financial status had dwindled to £3.45.

I blew 36p on a Mars Bar and sat on the bench outside the Library trying to make it last. Once my energy cells were partially recharged, I decided to walk some of the way back to Chiswick. If I paced myself correctly, I could time it so that it would appear to Maggie that I had been in school all day. And, I'd pass quite a number of fare stages at any rate.

I headed down the road towards World's End. I had passed Henry J Beans and American Classics and was just pausing, because walking that far on a Mars Bar had brought on a serious stitch when, bent double outside a large Chemist and Hardware Store, I set eyes on the answer to my financial problems. Four minutes later I had rashly invested three pounds and nine pence and equipped myself for a brand new career:

'VISION OPTIMISER – AUTOMOTIVES
For those who enjoy being on the move and meeting
new people.
Outdoor life – Flexible hours.'

The only thing I had to do now was select the traffic lights at which to site my new enterprise.

*

I vaguely remembered from my former, happier life, sitting in the car, with Mummy fuming at this really massive inter-section where the Earl's Court Road crosses the Cromwell Road. It's on the way to and from virtually everywhere and the traffic lights take forever to change. So I headed up there.

I dropped off to fill up my bucket with nice warm water in McDonalds' loos. On my way out I had an embarrassing contretemps with the manager who tried to confiscate my bucketful. Honestly, the stinginess of some people! As I pointed out, it was only tap water, not Perrier, for godsake. That manager would live to regret his outburst. I swore, then and there, I would never let another McDonald's hamburger pass my lips.

Once I arrived at the intersection, I waited for a moment in order to study the form of the traffic passing by. It was a toss-up really. The Earls Court Road traffic was a pretty mixed bunch of commercial vehicles and Sloaney mummies ferrying shopping and kids and dogs down south. The Cromwell Road lot were a load of business travellers, inter-mixed with buses and limos and taxis heading to and from Heathrow. I decided that the westbound traffic on the Cromwell Road looked marginally better-heeled – or thicker-treaded – and positioned myself in readiness by the lights.

I wondered if Pavarotti felt like this before he went on stage . . . My first business transaction was a bit of a failure actually. This really massive container lorry drew up at the lights and I waved my squeegee and shouted, 'Want your windscreen washed?'

'Sure . . .' said the driver, with a grin. 'Feel free!'

I hauled myself up on to the footplate and leaned over. The bonnet of the lorry was vast and even stretching as far as I could, I only managed to reach a tiny bit of windscreen.

The guys in the cab were having a high old time giving me advice, and then the driver put on the windscreen wash and I got soaked. I climbed down, icy water running down my neck and into my sweatshirt.

'Thanks,' shouted the driver and the lorry took off belching diesel fumes over me.

After that I had a stream of blokes talking to their mobile phones who shook their heads and glared at me. And then one nice sympathetic lady who actually smiled and said, 'Could you be an absolute angel and do my wing mirrors too?'

She gave me 5p – 5p for back, front and two wing mirrors!

After that a van came along that hadn't been washed since it left the factory.

'Can you do the rear windows, mate?'

It would have helped to have had a ladder to do it but I made a pretty good job and received 20p.

Half an hour or so of job experience behind me and I was starting to be able to judge with a professional eye the kind of drivers who would cough up.

The worst were the kind who lacked any sense of motoring pride: vans and clapped-out Fords with things like 'Please clean me' and 'Dirt testing, do not disturb' written with a finger in their grime.

A car with a jacket hanging from a hook inside was generally a good bet. I guess the drivers were mostly reps and understood the value of honest toil in a harsh economic climate.

Flash cars like Mercedes and Porsches were a total gamble. One guy gave me a pound coin. Another asked me if I took American Express and a third let me wash his windscreen and then told me to 'Piss off'.

After an hour or so, I reckon I had totted up about £2.90, so I had practically broken even and recouped my initial investment, when this vast limo with blacked-out windows drew up. A uniformed chauffeur sat at the wheel and studiously ignored me.

I didn't even bother to raise my squeegee at him and I was just heading for the car behind when a rear electronic window silently slid down a crack and a voice from under a kind of checked tea-towel said: 'Excuse me. Could you oblige me by cleaning my back window?'

There was hardly a speck on it, but I gave it the once-over anyway.

A hand appeared through the crack.

'Thank you so much. I'm leaving the country actually, so you might as well have my loose change,' said the voice.

The window slid down an inch further, the hand emerged, opened and let a stream of coins pour into mine.

As the car drove off I stared in disbelief at the pile of coins in my cupped hands. There must have been nearly ten quid!

I felt pretty euphoric after that. By around 4.00 pm the traffic was starting to build up, swelled by mummies on school runs and I was racing from car to car like a maniac. I was just running my squeegee over the rear window of a Range Rover, to the intense interest of a couple of Rottweilers who were slavering at the mouth and barking fit to burst, when I noticed that I was being watched.

A massive bloke, in a grimy T-shirt and ripped jeans, was standing with another stubble-faced guy with a spotted handkerchief tied round his head pirate-fashion. I just finished the Rottweilers' car with a professional flick of grimy water over the rear offside bumper when they moved in.

'Watcha think yer doing?' asked the big bloke.

The answer to this question seemed pretty obvious so I bent over my bucket and pretended to be busy cleaning out my squeegee. Then I noticed that they were both wearing the official regalia of windscreen washers – the filthy rag attached to the belt.

The big bloke was waving his squeegee at me threateningly. It was a huge industrial model. I rose to my full height.

He gestured contemptuously towards my little red plastic one.

'This is my pitch, right? 'Op it!'

The boy with the scarf round his head flexed his squeegee threateningly.

'You 'eard. Move!' he added.

There didn't seem to be an awful lot of point in arguing with them. And, come to think of it, I had been about to call it a day anyway. So I emptied my bucket into the gutter, 'accidentally' slopping some rat-grey water over the bigger bloke's sneakers, and 'opped it -- very fast.

On the way back on the bus to Chiswick, I emptied my pockets into the bucket and counted my takings – £14.79p! Not a bad afternoon's work.

I decided to blow it all making it up to Chuck for the money he'd lashed out on me.

'Hey, Chuck . . .' I said racing up the stairs.

He was busy lying on his bunk staring into space.

'Fancy taking in a film tonight? Your choice. My treat?'

Chuck turned on to his side and eyed me doubtfully.

'What with?'

I shoved the bucket full of coins under his nose.

'Been collecting for "Wildlife" outside Sainsbury's?' he asked.

'No, I earned it,' I said.

I explained about the Classifieds and the phone calls and how enlightenment had come when I caught sight of my red squeegee rising like Excalibur from a sea of bin-liners in the Hardware Store window.

But Chuck wasn't concentrating. He suddenly interrupted saying: 'Classifieds, that's it! That's how we'll find her!'

'Who?'

'Julie. You know, like Madonna in *Desperately Seeking Susan*. We'll advertise for her.'

Chuck was already rifling through his schoolbag for a pen and paper.

It was so simple I wondered why I hadn't thought of it earlier.

Within minutes we had composed the ad:

'ALTERNATIVE REALITY' DESPERATELY SEEK-
ING JULIE. RING 0181 749 6053. MATTER OF LIFE
OR DEATH.

We had quite a long discussion about where we should place it. I favoured the *Telegraph* because Mummy had always said that 'simply everyone' read their Personal Column, but Chuck wasn't so sure.

In the end we settled for *Time Out*. It had the right kind of wacky flavour, it hung around for a week, and a little research established that it cost less too.

I dialled the number of *Time Out*.

'*Time Out* Classifieds. Can I help you?' answered a voice.

'Can I place an ad in next week's edition?' I said.

'What was it you want to advertise, Caller?'

'I'm trying to find a woman.'

'We have a standard rate for Teledating at just £29.50,' said the voice.

I was shocked. 'Not for a date. I'm looking for just one particular woman,' I said.

There was a slight pause.

'Maybe you should try an Introductions Agency,' the voice suggested.

'You don't understand,' I was getting quite het up. 'I know the person I want to find – she's called Julie – we've just lost contact.'

'Oh, in that case you want "Messages". I'll transfer you.'

Eventually, we established that the ad would go in next Wednesday's *Time Out* provided we could get twenty-five quid to the *Time Out* office by the end of the week.

'That puts the wraps on our evening out,' said Chuck.

'Rubbish!' I said. 'That's two whole days away. I'll easily make £25.00 by then.'

So we went to the cinema. Actually, I was a bit surprised that Casper and Maggie were so lax on a term time evening. I mean, my mother nearly has a fit if I so much as drop off for tea on my way home. I suppose it would be uncharitable to suggest that my parents' concern is anything to do with the fact they have to fork out for the fees. Anyway, Maggie didn't even enquire whether we'd done our homework. Neither did she ask when we were getting back. This was the life!

The film Chuck chose to see, *Death Watch*, was a new release, only on at the Chelsea MGM. So when we got there we had to queue for about twenty minutes. Our tickets came to twelve pounds, but I was glad to be able to splash out with my well-earned wealth. The effect was slightly spoilt by the time it took for the ticket lady to count the money. And some wag behind us had the cheek to suggest that I should take the hat down the queue again while she was at it.

Anyway, I gave Chuck my last handful of coins and he went to join the popcorn queue.

Having secured our tickets, I was making my way through the foyer to find Chuck when I came face to face with . . . *me.*

I think we were both caught a bit off guard.

'Have you come to see a film?' she stammered.

'That's the general idea.' (It was a pretty daft question, we were in a cinema, for godsake.)

'I mean,' she said, blushing scarlet, 'have you come to see *Death Watch*?'

It was the end of the school holidays and the other two

films showing were *The Return of Dumbo* and *Care Bears go to the Seaside*.

'Well, yes, as a matter of fact,' I said.

'So have we.'

'Really?'

The other half of 'we' appeared at that moment.

'Oh, hi!' said Franz. 'Who's this then, Justine?' (Very meaningfully) 'Aren't you going to introduce us?'

This was bi-*zarre*. Here I was being introduced by *myself* to *my very best friend*!'

Justine was getting oddly flustered.

'Where are you sitting?' demanded Franz.

Our tickets said Row F. The girls, who had booked by phone earlier, were in Row G.

'That's a pity,' I said, trying to play the part of the polite male.

'Well, maybe we could meet up afterwards,' said Franz.

'Maybe,' I said.

Chuck had just got to the end of the popcorn queue as the girls were disappearing into the auditorium. He headed after them, spewing popcorn as he did so.

The lights were going down as we got inside and Chuck tripped over a couple of people, trying to catch up with the girls. I hauled him back and got him seated in his correct seat. So he had to content himself with the only physical contact being intermittent bombardments of popcorn for the duration of the film. I don't think we made ourselves wildly popular with the rest of the audience. But the girls took all this attention for the compliment it was no doubt meant to be.

After the film, we bumped into them again in the crowd jostling to get out through the foyer.

'Do you fancy going for a coffee?' asked Franz.

Chuck was about to say yes but I stood on his foot

and said: 'No, I think we'd better be off actually. School tomorrow, you know.'

Franz raised an eyebrow.

'Got to get your beauty sleep?'

I glanced at Justine.

She was blushing again.

(*I just couldn't figure out why she was behaving like such a wimp.*)

'I'd have liked a coffee, as a matter of fact,' said Chuck as the girls walked off down the street.

'Number one, we haven't enough cash left,' I pointed out. 'And number two, believe it or not, I actually find it just the teeniest bit difficult, coming face to face with *myself* everywhere I go.'

Nine

The next morning Chuck got up and looked out of the window and said, 'Oh, my God.'

'What's wrong?' I asked, sitting up and banging my head on the ceiling as usual.

'It's raining.'

'Not to worry,' I said, settling myself back on the pillows. 'You can lend me a mac or something. I'm not going to let a little rain put me off.'

Chuck muttered something that sounded like 'Windscreen Wipers' and headed for the shower.

I suddenly realized the significance of what he had said: *windscreen wipers*!

I hit my head on the ceiling again.

I leaped out of bed, met the floor with the full force of eleven stone and hobbled towards the window.

The rain had a well-settled-in look about it.

I searched the sky fruitlessly for fragments of thinning cloud or maybe just a sample strip of blue. All up above was flat relentless grey.

Nobody ever stops to wonder where Windscreen Washers go when it rains. It's one of those unsolved mysteries of the universe, like where shop assistants go when you want to return something, or where all the truffle disappears to in foie gras.

Anyway, this one went shopping. Well, *looking* at any rate. I suppose it was from sheer force of habit. But the comforting warmth of Harrods beckoned. I selected the smartest carrier bag I could find from Maggie's hoard. I have a feeling it might have come with purchases from Oxfam because it had a kind of 'pre-owned' look about it but it was a Liberty one at any rate.

Then, once I had retrieved my bucket and squeegee from under the Davis' hedge, I set out for Knightsbridge.

I never realized before what an alien world a department store presents to the male. I started the tour with my custom-ary circuit of the testers in the Perfume Hall. Assistants, trapped behind their counters with that strained, captive look over-moisturized skin gives you, eyed me warily.

A massive L'Egoiste bottle caught my eye. Written beneath it was the message:

He walks on the positive side of that fine line separating arrogance from an awareness of his self-worth.

I considered this for a moment. It was quite some claim for the average guy who only wanted to smell good. But in deference to my current gender, I allowed the assistant to give me a generous waft of it all the same.

After that I had a good snoop through the clothes in Way In and found this absolutely stunning black dress which was precisely the thing I had been searching for for months and months. Honestly, seriously, it was divine. It was black velvet with a massive slit up to the thigh, lined throughout and cut just off the shoulder . . . It was stunning! And I couldn't even try it on! It was so frustrating! It was my size, too and they only had one size ten left. I took it over to a mirror and sort of held it against me trying to imagine what it would look like once I was back to the real me.

'Can I help you?'

An assistant had popped up from nowhere.

'I was just wondering what it would look like on . . . I mean, on my girlfriend.'

'Why don't you bring her in to try it. It's our late night tonight.'

My mind was racing.

The dress was sooo gorgeous and I should just be able to afford it, provided Justine hadn't splurged all my birthday money in the meantime.

'Would you like me to keep it on one side for you?'

I considered. It was gorgeous. And it was the last size ten! Oh indecision!

'OK, right. I'll try and get her to come along,' I said.

I had made my way down the escalator to the ground floor and was checking the weather – it was still raining – when I suddenly realized that in the heat of the moment I had mislaid my carrier bag.

I shot up again in the lift and started to search Way In, groping through the massed ranks of designer wear. The bag was nowhere to be seen. This was serious, man. I mean, my whole livelihood could be going up the spout.

I was checking under an aggressive row of Vivienne West-wood bustiers when a voice said: 'Lost something?' It was 'my' assistant again.

'Yes, a carrier bag. A Liberty one.'

'It's OK. It was handed in,' she said.

'Great.'

'It's been sent up to Lost Property, Fifth Floor.'

I trailed up to the Fifth Floor and joined the queue. The

woman in front of me was in a right old flap. She'd lost a diamond out of her engagement ring.

'Could you give me some sort of estimate of its value?'

I had no idea a single diamond could cost over £2000.

The man behind her had left his Louis Vuitton briefcase in the Gents. The carelessness of some people! Anyway, they were both asked to stand to one side and wait while enquiries were being made.

'Yes?' said the desk clerk, eyeing me superciliously.

'I've lost a carrier bag. A Liberty carrier bag in Way In,' I said.

'Could you describe the contents of this bag for me, please?'

Both the diamond lady and the Louis Vuitton man looked at me expectantly.

I leaned over the desk and lowered my voice.

'A bucket and a squeegee.'

'Pardon?' he said.

I cleared my throat and announced in my very best polished accent: 'A blue plastic bucket approximately fifteen inches in diameter and a red plastic double-sided squeegee.'

The bag was handed over without so much as a twitch.

'Would you mind signing for it please, Sir.'

I spent the rest of the day in Harrod's, my eyes glued to the floor. When all hope of either the diamond turning up or the weather clearing up had faded, I decided to head back to Chiswick.

It was something of a relief to reach 45, Ferndale Avenue and I was just making for the fridge when I met Maggie coming through the kitchen weighed down by several carrier bags bulging with booty destined for the bottle bank.

'Would you like some help with all that?' I asked, playing the considerate guest.

'Thank you, Jake, that's really nice of you. I would,' said Maggie. 'If you could load this lot into the car, I'll go back for more.'

After twenty minutes or so, the 2CV was positively splitting at the sides, crammed with packs of flattened card, bundles of newspapers, carriers of crushed cans and six bags of bottles.

'Right, let's go,' said Maggie.

I was just easing myself into what was left of the passenger seat when a voice said, 'Hi there!'

Justine was standing on the pavement. Actually, in a totally FREAKY kind of way, I was starting to get used to these constant confrontations. Weird as it may seem, one kind of settles into leading a *double* life.

'Can I help?' she asked.

'No room,' shouted Maggie over the buzz of the engine.

'Hi . . .' said Justine to me. I noticed she had put lashbuilder on really carefully. Each lash was standing out stiff and separate like the legs of a spider with rigor mortis.

'Why don't you go in and start making tea,' Maggie shouted. 'Chuck's not back yet. I've just made a parsnip and carrot cake.'

And then we whirred off down the road.

The bottle bank was at the main council dump, not far from the allotments. It was an equally desolate area haunted by screaming gulls and the occasional optimist sorting through the rubbish for anything of resale value. The rain really brought out its true character and its own most memorable smell.

'How are Justine and Chuck getting along?' Maggie asked as we sorted the brown bottles from the green, huddled under her umbrella.

'Fine,' I said. 'Why do you ask?'

'Just wondered,' said Maggie.

I shifted a second carrier out of the boot of the 2CV.

'Perhaps we should invite her to stay on for dinner,' she suggested.

'Maybe she's tied up tonight,' I replied. (You never knew, she might just have got her act together and be planning on dropping in on Alex to try a little bedside charming.)

'Maybe it'd be a bit too obvious?' said Maggie with a laugh.

'Obvious?' I said.

'Well, Chuck and Justine . . . you know.'

At this point I dropped a Gordon's Gin bottle into the clear glass container by mistake. A guilt-ridden vision of a million or so milk-bottles with just a hint-of-a-tint leaped to mind.

'Chuck and Justine' – what was Maggie getting at?

When we got back Chuck still hadn't arrived home.

'Did he say anything about staying on late?' asked Maggie, helping us to slabs of cake.

'Didn't see a lot of him today,' I said and added with a meaningful look towards Justine, 'Maybe he's stopped off to see poor Alex.'

Justine and Maggie then got into a discussion about what a terrific guy Alex was and how heroic he was being. I thought of him propped up in bed with that fixed grin of satisfaction on his face, and nearly choked on my cake.

Stalin dropped in halfway through tea and raced up to Justine who was making come-hither-cat noises and patting her lap. He was purring fit to bust and rubbing his neck against her legs. Then, catching sight of me, he kind of stopped in his tracks, shook himself and sat down with both ears back looking from one to the other of us, totally confused.

His appearance launched Maggie into a lengthy description of how Stalin had taken such a shine to me and then the phone rang and Maggie went to answer it.

There was a long silence. It was a god-given opportunity to try and find out how things stood with Alex, but I didn't know where to begin. I was dying to know if the Franz/Alex 'relationship' had really had it. And, if so, whether she was making well-founded plans to move in. Seriously, if Alex was currently 'single', and in a captive state like this in the Hospital, it could be the opportunity-of-a-lifetime to make her presence felt. If only I could get her to his bedside! I kept taking furtive sideways glances at her, trying to assess whether she was looking at her best . . . I mean, did she frankly stand a chance with him?

She caught me mid-glance and quickly looked away.

We both started talking at once.

'So how did you meet Chuck . . .?'

'How long have you known . . .?'

'Sorry, after you . . .'

'No, after you . . .'

After we'd established how long we'd each known Chuck, and dealt with such vital and highly charged issues as what we thought the weather was about to do, we lapsed into silence.

After a time she cleared her throat and said: 'What sign are you . . .?'

I stared at her in disbelief. I mean a question like that scores a double century on the naffness scale.

'Dunno . . . basically, not wildly interested in that sort of thing,' I said.

'When's your birthday?' she insisted.

That *she* should persist with a topic of such unparalleled tedium put me totally off guard. I was so absolutely gob-smacked that the date kind of slipped out automatically, before I could stop myself.

'Tenth of September.'

Justine slammed down her teacup and stared at me.

'But that's really freaky! I don't believe it! It's the same as mine . . . and Chuck's! You're joking! . . .'

(Perhaps, I ought to explain here that it's not such a total coincidence as it sounds. You see, my mother met Chuck's mother while we both were busy being born in Queen Charlotte's Hospital – so Chuck and I are kind of unrelated twins – or, correction, triplets!)

'Oh, it's not such a coincidence,' I said, trying to defuse the situation by launching into Maths-speak. 'It's a 1 in 365 chance or 366 if it's a leap year.'

'But to meet up, like this, three of us in a city full of millions of people?' she said. 'It's really weird! It must mean we've got masses in common!'

'Quite possibly,' I said. (Just *how* much might surprise her!)

Justine then launched into a deep intensive interrogation about my taste in films. And surprise, surprise! She and I happened to have seen much the same things!

'Doesn't it just go to show,' she said. 'All this stuff about the stars, there must be some truth in it. Mustn't there?'

(Her mind had conveniently blanked out the fact that Chuck preferred Arnold Schwarzenegger and Clint Eastwood movies, but maybe his stars were just that trifle less snugly conjoined than hers and mine.)

Maggie came back into the kitchen at that point.

'Have either of you two got anything planned for tonight?' she asked, rummaging through the fridge with a distracted air.

'Not really.' I shrugged and then let drop as casually as possible, 'How about visiting Alex?'

But oddly enough Justine didn't seem that interested.

'It's late night shopping,' she said. 'And I've got a clothing crisis on. Then I promised to catch up with Franz later.'

That's when I remembered the dress.

'Say, why don't we raid Harrod's?' I suggested.

Justine looked at me incredulously.

'Men hate shopping,' she said.

'I don't,' I said.

'Chuck does,' said Justine.

'All that conspicuous consumption and mindless materialism,' I said, imitating Chuck's 'socially committed' voice.

'Well, let's not wait for him,' said Justine. 'He's such a killjoy. We can always meet up later. I'm meeting Franz for a coffee. He could join us then.'

And so, leaving Maggie with a message for Chuck, the two of us set out for Harrod's.

Ten

I was right about the dress. It was wicked! It had been a bit tricky getting it from the assistant without Justine noticing. But while she was engrossed checking through a row of Kenzo, I shot off and then I kind of produced the dress with a flourish and said, 'How about this one?'

'Oh I don't know,' she said.

(*What did she mean, 'I don't know', this dress was brilliant, man!*)

'Go on! Try it on! I bet you'll look fantastic in it,' I said.

'Do you really think so?'

'Umm!!!'

'Well . . .' (checking the label) ' . . . it is my size, but . . . you don't think it's a bit . . . you know . . . the slit and everything?'

'No . . . not at all. It's really nice. Go on. Try it.'

'I'm not sure . . .'

I was practically on the point of grabbing her by the scruff of the neck and shoving her into the changing room when she said. 'Oh, all right then . . .'

After a few minutes, she came out and did a little twirl. Actually it looked somewhat odd with baseball boots and woolly socks on.

I studied her critically.

'It's OK . . .' I said doubtfully.

'You have to imagine it in heels,' she said standing on tiptoes and studying her reflection in the mirror with her head on one side.

Oh my god. In actual fact, from the back, I have to admit, it made *my bottom look big* – it really did.

'I like it,' she said.

'Well, you probably know best. I mean boys can't judge really . . .' I stalled, just praying she'd take the hint.

She didn't.

'You're a genius,' she said. 'Really honestly, I've been looking for a dress like this for months.'

(*She was telling me!*)

'I'll take it,' she said to the assistant.

Oh boy, there went a hundred and five quid. She wrote out the cheque there and then.

The dress was wrapped up in white crunchy tissue paper and put in a Way In carrier bag.

'Come on,' she said, leading the way. But we didn't get past the display of shoes.

'Oh look,' said Justine, holding up a pair of black shoes with the latest heel.

I took one from her and glanced at the price. They were £85. Eighty-five quid!!!

'They're fabulous,' she said.

(OK, now I was getting the picture. Flushed with the success of one purchase, the floodgates were open. She was losing all sense of judgement. She'd bought something. *Anything* could happen from now on.)

'They're pretty expensive,' I countered.

'Yes, but feel the leather. And they're perfect for the dress . . .'

'Haven't you already got a pair that would do?'

(*She must remember, she had a perfectly good pair of black shoes in the wardrobe, she only bought them three months ago, they'd hardly been worn for godsake!*)

'No . . .' she said, shaking her head. 'Nothing that would go with the dress.'

As luck would have it they hadn't run out of *my* size and I watched despondently as Justine paraded up and down in them. I was trying desperately to remember what my last bank balance had been.

'Won't all this make you overdrawn?' I suggested.

'Most probably,' she said as she signed the cheque with a flourish. 'But who cares? Let's face it, one only has one life to live.'

Which in the circumstances was a very unfortunate comment.

I trailed after her, carrying the bags, as we made for the café where we'd arranged to meet Chuck and Franz.

'Hang on a mo,' said Justine and she paused at a Midland Cash Dispenser. 'I'd better get some dosh out before those Harrod's cheques go through.'

I looked on as she took out her (actually *my*!) cash card and helped herself to £30 and a balance slip. I craned over her shoulder to see the balance slip which she screwed up and threw in the bin without so much as a glance. Thirty pounds of my money! No, hang on – correction. Thirty pounds of the *bank's* money!

By the time we reached Train Bleu (a rather exorbitant neo-French café that had recently opened in the King's Road) Chuck and Franz were already seated at a fake-scratched table in the window waiting for us.

Justine squeezed herself onto the bench seat beside me, then looked around with a smile and said, 'So what's everyone having. It's on me, OK?'

(*Hang on a minute! Here was tight-fisted me, blowing my money on a wally like Chuck, a taker like Franz and a boy she hardly knew. Something was seriously UP!*)

'Right!' said Franz running an expert finger down the list of cocktails. 'Let's all get smashed.'

'Oh well, er, Chuck's got school tomorrow. Better not kill off too many of his precious brain cells . . .' I started.

But in the end they all ordered vastly expensive cocktails while I had a measly cappuccino.

'So what have you been up to?' asked Franz, sucking through her straw and eyeing me over the salted rim of her glass. 'Rumour has it you weren't in school today.'

So I was being 'talked about' was I? I felt rather flattered actually.

'Jake's dropped out,' said Chuck. 'But whatever you do, don't tell Maggie and Casper.'

Chuck was passing around the Marlboros and before my amazed eyes Justine took one, lit up rather inexpertly from Franz's lighter and blew smoke over my coffee.

I just managed to stop myself reminding her that she'd given up. Geesus, those were my lungs she was treating with such lack of concern! So I gave her a long, hard, meaningful look instead. Justine stared back and then lowered her eyes.

'So if you've dropped out of school, what are you doing?' she asked, taking another life-threatening drag.

'I'm setting up my own busines, actually,' I said truthfully. Both girls looked impressed.

'Where did you get the capital?' asked Justine, taking an 'intelligent' interest.

'Errm, well . . . Mauritius mainly.'

'Kind of off-shore funds?' said Justine, looking dead impressed. She was getting in very deep water here. What she didn't know was that I knew that she didn't have the faintest idea what she was talking about. But then, nor did I . . .

'What does it involve exactly?' asked Franz.

Fortunately, Chuck who was obviously feeling rather left out of the conversation, interrupted at that point, by saying:

'What did you think of the film last night?'

Neither of the girls seemed to have heard him. They had latched into a deep SWOT analysis of my career potential. I was desperately trying to steer the conversation away from my past or my future – and actually even talking about my present was riddled with pitfalls.

So I took the cue from Chuck and repeated, 'So what did you think of the film?'

Magically, this became a riveting subject of debate. When we'd exhausted that, they all thought they'd like another cocktail.

I dug Chuck in the ribs.

'Don't worry,' said Justine. 'I've got thirty quid on me. We might as well blow it.'

(Might as well blow it! After the way she's been splurging at Way In. This was my overdraft she was referring to. This was really painful, man. I had to sit there passively non-smoking and sipping lukewarm cappuccino while she blew my money, my brain cells and ruined my lungs as well.)

By the time we left the café, they had totted up a bill of £24.50. Justine paid up without turning a hair. She even added a £2.50 tip! I watched helplessly as the saucer with the money on it was being borne away. Chuck was very quiet on the way back to Chiswick. I don't think the cocktails had been a very good idea, he'd have been better sticking to Grolsch. When we got to the house he shot up the stairs double-quick and headed for the bathroom.

Huh! Can't take the booze, I thought to myself.

I left a tactful interlude and then I went up after him.

When I reached the bathroom door, I found it was locked. And there was the most god-awful row coming from inside. It sounded as though someone was kicking the towel rail very hard. I stood outside and listened. It could only be Chuck in there. He sounded as if he'd gone berserk.

'You all right?' I shouted through the door.

'What's it to you?'

I paused. I'd never been spoken to like that before by Chuck. His voice sounded kind of weird.

I waited, the kicking noise subsided and there was the sound of the taps being turned on hard.

'You going to be long?' I called.

Chuck threw the bathroom door open and stood in the doorway glaring at me. His eyes were all bloodshot. He looked as if he'd been crying – but boys don't cry, do they?

'Anything wrong?'

Chuck pushed past me and went into the bedroom. He hauled a sports holdall out from under his bed and silently started cramming clothes into it.

'You moving out or something?' I asked.

'No, you are,' he said.

'Me? Why? What have I done?'

'I just don't think it's very funny, that's all.'

'What is?'

'All that eye-contact.'

'Eye-contact?'

'Justine . . . for godsake. To have to sit and watch all that blatant bloody body language. I suppose you think it's funny . . .'

'Hey, Chuck. Cool it! What's up?'

He paused from stuffing socks into the holdall and looked me full in the face.

'Can't you see she's really got the hots for you?'

I sat down on the bed. I didn't know whether to laugh or pretend to take him seriously.

'Don't be ridiculous!' I said.

'Ridiculous! I saw the way she was looking at you. Franz and I had to sit waiting for hours while you were both having it away in Harrod's or wherever you were. *Geesus!*'

At that point I couldn't help it. I burst out laughing. I

realize that this was totally the wrong thing to do in the circumstances, but I simply couldn't stop myself.

Chuck zipped the bag shut and threw it at me.

'You can't be serious,' I said, trying to get my breath back, fighting to control myself.

'Why not? You must admit you're loving it, lapping it up, leading her on.'

'Leading her on. How? Boy, aren't you forgetting something. Like *who* I am? What do you think I am, man? – a pervert or something?'

(Boy, this was totally *bizarre*. Chuck seemed to have totally lost sight of the facts. Just because I looked like a male he was starting to treat me as one. In fact, as things stood, it seemed that – in a totally sinister way – he had actually begun to regard me as one. Maybe he really thought I was stuck like this, for good! Nightmare!)

'Well?'

Chuck shrugged and started stabbing at his computer keyboard for comfort.

'I just don't think it's working out – you staying here, that's all.'

'Come on . . . loosen up . . . what is all this?'

'Didn't you notice the way those girls were acting. *Both* of them!'

'No . . . how?'

'Like you were *GOD* or something.'

'What rot! They were just being friendly. Geesus! I do believe you're jealous!'

'I think it would be better if you left,' said Chuck, in a dry, strained voice.

'Where am I supposed to go?'

'What's it to me? Frankly, I don't care,' he swung round on his office chair so he had his back to me.

I watched him in disbelief. He was really upset. He had found his packet of Marlboros and was lighting one.

'Anyway,' I said, trying to think of something which would calm him down. 'You can take it from me, Justine couldn't be less interested in me . . . Surely you've noticed, haven't you? – Alex is the one she's nuts about.'

'Alex!' exclaimed Chuck.

'Yes . . . Alex!'

'You're having me on . . . she's got more sense.'

I shook my head. 'I should know, for godsake!'

'But, Alex!' said Chuck. 'That dickhead. Get real!'

'He's got his good points . . .' I said, huffily.

That's when I caught sight of Chuck's face reflected in his Apple Mac screen. He *had* been crying. He was a bit now, actually.

And then I remembered the photos in the drawer and what Maggie had hinted at at the bottle bank and I felt a real jerk. Because, even though Chuck is a real wally, he's a great guy. He's about the best friend I've ever had, for godsake.

'Don't,' I said, and instinctively I went and put an arm across his shoulders.

Chuck wiped his face on his sleeve and swung round, 'Take your hands off me,' he said.

We sat in silence for a bit and then Chuck got up and took the bag from me and slowly unpacked it and put everything back in the drawers.

Men! I thought. Talk about jumping to conclusions. Just because the girls were kind of friendly and liked me – we'd got a lot in common for godsake. Honestly, *men*! . . . poor sods . . . ruled by their bodies, of course. I came to the conclusion that Chuck was being blinded by rampant male sexuality – sad case . . .

Later that night, when we were both in bed, I lay in the top bunk staring at the ceiling, turning the whole thing over in my mind. Actually I was starting to feel really, really guilty. I mean, now I knew how Chuck felt about me, I realized how badly I had treated him. I went through all the times I had stood him up or rung him up and made some transparent excuse because I'd had a better offer. God, how could I have been such a heartless cow? I was trying desperately to formulate in my mind some way of explaining, of making it all up to him.

'Chuck?' I said.

He kind of grunted in reply. He was obviously still very upset.

I cleared my throat. Actually this was one of the hardest statements I've ever had to make.

'I really do care about you, you know.'

He was silent. I think maybe he was a bit overcome.

'You're the very best friend I've ever had,' I went on. 'Probably the best friend I'll ever have. And that's kind of more than just fancying guys and all that kind of thing.'

This was really difficult to say.

'I mean, over the past few days, I've really started to realize what a great guy you are. I mean, I guess it's a very special kind of relationship, you know, not needing anything in return . . . like we do . . . I mean . . . like we don't . . .'

I paused.

' . . . and Chuck?'

He still didn't respond, so I leaned over and looked down into his bunk to see how he was taking all this.

Chuck was lying in bed with his eyes closed and his Walkman on full blast.

I could have killed him!

Eleven

The next morning I woke up to find something very curious indeed had happened to my face. I rubbed an enquiring hand over it and it made a noise like fine sandpaper.

I climbed out of my bunk and made for the bathroom. Having locked the door, I examined my chin in the mirror.

Gross! You're not going to believe this but, *I needed a shave.*

I adjusted the light over the mirror. It wasn't the kind of designer stubble one would normally associate with a hunk of my status, it was a light thin covering with a lot of sparse patches like a lawn during a hose-ban.

I steeled myself and reached for Casper's Old Spice shaving foam. Having got myself up to look like Father Christmas, I decided I couldn't quite face Casper's razor which was propped up between the toothbrushes, caked with old shaving foam and sprouting aggressive-looking hairs, so I used Maggie's little pink ladies' razor instead.

I don't think it could have been wildly sharp because by the time I'd finished, I felt like a victim of cosmetic skin-peeling. I splashed on aftershave and nearly hit the ceiling.

Back in the bedroom, I found Chuck shaving himself in comfort with a battery shaver. I had no idea Chuck was into shaving.

He grunted at me and signalled to keep quiet. He was listening to the weather forecast.

' . . . *widespread showers are forecast all over the British Isles, winds will reach gale force in the south-east. No let-up is expected in the poor weather conditions until after the weekend* . . .'

The voice continued with callous indifference to my destiny. I went to the window and stared out. A thin steady rain was falling.

'Oh boy . . .' I said.

Chuck switched off his razor and gazed at the rain.

'You're going to have to find some way of getting that £25.00 to *Time Out* by the end of the day,' he said. 'Otherwise, I'm telling you – you're out of here. OK?'

Then he looked a little amazed at himself for his masterful tone of voice and added, 'Maybe you could borrow it from yourself?'

I shook my head.

'Justine blew it all last night. Maybe if you hadn't all had a second cocktail . . .'

'No excuses,' Chuck interrupted. 'Either that ad goes in or it's cardboard city for you tonight, mate.'

No more was said. Chuck headed off for school and I was left to solve the problem.

Geesus. This was heavy, man. Surely Chuck couldn't be heartless enough to leave me to fend for myself, could he? I mean these days he genuinely seemed to be callous enough to think he could treat me as an equal! There was none of the cushy treatment I'd been used to as a girl – all those delicate enquiries as to whether I was suffering from stomach cramps or was likely to get molested. I mean, he was even getting to the stage when he didn't care if he scratched or farted in front of me – gross! The sooner I regained my proper sexual status the better.

I lay in the top bunk turning all this over in my mind,

gazing at the ceiling and trying to gain inspiration from its random pattern of hairline cracks.

Maggie put her head round the door.

'Not going to school? Not well? Can I get you a camomile tea or a garlic capsule or something?'

'Thanks, but I'm OK. I've got "frees", that's all.'

Maggie frowned. 'Well, you aren't going to get much study done lying there like that, are you?'

God! She was starting to sound like Mummy.

'And incidentally . . .'

'Yes?'

'You might chase up Air India, they're being very slack.'

'Sure . . . I'll get on to them.'

Anyway, I took the hint and climbed out of bed and ran a bath.

In the bath I did some pretty fundamental thinking and came to absolutely no conclusion at all.

I was still deep in thought when Maggie rattled on the doorknob.

'Phone call for you!'

'Hang on, I'll take it,' I shouted and reached for a towel. These days a phone call was quite an event in my life.

I took the call on the upstairs phone.

'Hi,' said a voice. It was *me*.

'Oh hi,' I said.

'What are you up to today?'

'Oh well, I was planning a few business deals but I don't think the climate is quite right for anything major at the moment.'

'So you've got time on your hands?' Her voice sounded all kind of bright and hopeful.

Water was running down my legs and forming a puddle on the landing carpet.

'Quite possibly. Why do you ask?'

'I was thinking of going over to the Club for a swim and a

sauna and maybe a sunbed – wondered if you'd like to come along?'

Now, Mummy had just enrolled me into this really pricey Health and Leisure Club. I had hardly used it yet. It was a tempting invitation. And come to think of it, I had to find somewhere to spend the day. I could always keep one eye on the weather . . .

'I guess I could manage it as long as I can keep within reach of a phone,' I said.

'No problems, I'll meet you there.'

Justine gave detailed instructions on how to get to the Club on the wrong bus and then rang off.

I squelched back to the bathroom, and as I was drying myself, I pondered on what Daddy called 'the essential unfairness of life'. 'Don't expect life to be fair, Justine. It's not and it never can be.'

Looking at it from the Cheyne Walk point of view this had appeared to be a sad philosophical truth about the world which one simply had to accept. Viewed from 45, Ferndale Avenue with the jaded eye of a weather-bound windscreen washer 'life's essential unfairness' looked more like pure bloody injustice.

Well, at least if I was going to end up curled up in cardboard tonight, I was going to be squeaky-clean and lightly tanned.

Justine's Health and Leisure Club was set in landscaped grounds in a nice quiet West London suburb. I waited for her in the shelter of the gatehouse and watched the Norland nannies by the lake instructing their small damp charges in the basics of charity work – distributing bread to the ducks.

Justine was the standard half-hour late which meant I had plenty of time to study the latest in duck behaviour. I also indulged in going over in my mind just how much money she had splurged the day before and working out precisely how overdrawn she must have made me. Curiously enough, one of the few compensations of being male was that purely mechanical brain functions, like mental arithmetic, seemed to have taken on a new lease of life. I could actually picture that little black number on the bank statement with the minus sign beside it, it was £93.52. She was going to have to try and get round Daddy again to bale her out. This could be tricky. Daddy had been pretty hard to handle lately. He was using the 'Recession' as a shield against practically everything.

I considered other possible avenues of income. If only I had been prudent enough to have made some sort of investments. And then suddenly I had this vision of a very ancient and dog-eared Post Office Savings Certificate Book. Yonks and yonks ago, before Jemima (my sister) and I had discovered the salutary effect of a good healthy spending spree, we had been encouraged to save our Christmas and Birthday money.

At the time I had derived some perverse sort of pleasure from sticking those little certificates into the book and counting them. I must have hoarded at least a hundred pounds worth of certificates in the book . . . but where on earth had I put it? I hadn't seen it in years . . .

I was interrupted from this important train of thought by a 'Hi . . . been here long?'

Justine had turned up wearing her very best new skin-tight black leather trousers. She had made a real effort with her hair too. I wondered why on earth she had bothered. She was only going for a swim.

'Hi,' I said and gave her a peck on each cheek as it was offered. This felt really weird, man!

'So you found it all right?'

The answer to this seemed to be fairly self-evident so I ignored the question and said:

'Have you heard how Alex is coming along?'

'They've operated and apparently he's survived,' she said. She was most obviously trying to sound laid back and uninterested, you know the way people do when they *really fancy someone.*

'So when will he be up and about?' I probed.

'Rumour has it, they're letting him out today. Why?'

'Just wondered how he and Franz were getting on, that's all.'

'Oh, she still thinks he's a prat,' she said.

I waited for her to amplify on this but she didn't. In fact, it was the same all that morning. I was just dying for a long, informative girlie gossip with all the ins-and-outs of the Alex situation – the more scandalous elements brought vividly to life with all the vital details intact – but it seemed my new sexual status excluded me from all that.

We started the morning in a rather dehydrating fashion with a sunbed each, followed by a sauna. We took it in turns to make mercy dashes to the iced water dispenser.

During one of these breaks I took the opportunity to ring Maggie and put her mind at ease about the luggage.

'Hello . . . Maggie Davis speaking.'

I dropped into my best Bombay Mix accent.

'Could I speak to Mr Jake Drake, please?' (OK, I know – the name was Chuck's fault, said it kind of gave me some sort of nautical heritage.)

'I'm sorry, he's not here at the moment, can I take a message?'

'This is Air India calling, a most regrettable incident has overcome his personal effects . . .'

'Oh dear . . .'

'They have been misdirected to Gander, Newfoundland.'

'Oh *dear* . . . So when will they be back?'

'Most unfortunately not at all. Due to a suspect package

they have been most totally destroyed in a controlled explosion.'

'How dreadful.'

'Our company, of course, will fully recompense him.'

'I see.'

I could see Justine emerging from the sauna in search of her iced water, so I hurriedly drew the conversation to a close.

'Lloyds will be in touch, goodbye.'

'Everything all right?' Justine asked, offering me a sip.

'Fine. Got a bit of an insurance panic on, that's all.'

I managed quite successfully to avoid answering any difficult questions of a business nature by suggesting a swim.

The Club has this massive new indoor pool flanked by artificial ferns and other exotic vegetation to make it look kind of tropical to match the general temperature of the place, and to keep the Club members from pining for the Bahamas.

Well-steamed and medium-browned, I had changed into Chuck's Bermudas which, although I say it myself, looked one-helluva-lot better on me. I considered the effect in the changing room mirror. I'd kind of kept the same proportions as my previous self, long legs, etc, but what had been redistributed had certainly gone to all the right places. I took a look at myself sideways – not bad, that's what they call a six-pack, man!

All the same, I paused at the changing room door before making my entrance and made a fundamental and little-known discovery about the male of the species. No matter how brilliantly their body is built, cruelly exposed in swimwear, they feel just as self-conscious and unconfident as we do. I took a deep breath, flexed my muscles and, parting the plastic palms with the practised casualness of Tarzan, I made my entrance.

Justine gave me a swift, appraising glance and was visibly

impressed. I must admit this made me feel a whole lot better. So I hammed it up a bit playing the 'aquatic male'. By some instinctive programmed behaviour, I suddenly found I was doing a lot of showy diving in from the side and a splashy crawl from end to end. Actually, it was pretty exhilarating having the extra muscle power, and I really entered into the spirit of the whole thing, swimming underneath Justine and popping up in front of her, etc. She had her hair bunched up on top with a butterfly clip in a futile attempt to keep it dry and was doing a fair amount of tame head-out-of-the-water breaststroke, making screaming noises whenever I approached. So I did what was expected of me and ducked her. It was all pretty predictable stuff.

Later, when we were both wrapped in towels and laid out on a couple of loungers sipping Coke, I at last got her back on to the vital subject of *Alex*.

'So how was Alex when you last saw him?'

'Fine.'

'In good spirits?'

'Umm, yes actually.'

'He's not cut up or anything about Franz not visiting?'

'Oh no . . . that's ancient history.' I waited for her to go on but she just sucked concentratedly on her straw.

'So did you have him all to yourself?'

'Not exactly . . . the last time I was in there, there was this really gross North Thames girl. She was all over him like a rash.'

(This was bad news, man. She sounded quite resigned to the situation – surely she wasn't going to give up the fight?)

'He talked quite a lot about you when Chuck and I saw him,' I countered.

She looked at me in a gratified manner over her straw which was making slurping noises as she reached the bottom of the Coke.

'Really?' she said, putting down the glass and preparing to be flattered. 'What did he say, precisely?'

At that point an unfortunate echo of Alex's voice came back to me: '*Bimbettes – do me a favour.*'

'I'm not sure if I can quite recall the actual words.'

'But the gist of it?'

'Well, it was something that clearly indicated that he thought you were highly desirable.'

'Really!'

She lay back on her lounger and closed her eyes – blissfully. I hoped I hadn't given her a false sense of security.

'Of course, it's hard to tell what Alex really thinks. He comes out with that kind of stuff about a load of women,' I backtracked.

Justine frowned and sat up.

'So give a girl some guidance – what *does* Alex go for, precisely?'

(How does one tactfully indicate to a girl like Justine that she really has to *go for it* – basically up until now she'd obviously been playing it far too cool.)

'Well, I think he likes the kind of girl who, kind of, puts herself about a bit . . .'

'Really . . .?'

'Umm . . . basically he doesn't give a damn what a girl looks like or . . .'

'He doesn't?

'He'd go for practically anything given the right signals . . . A guy like Alex likes a girl who clearly indicates she's available . . .'

'Like the Rash!' she said.

'Yeah kind of. But you're probably more his type.'

'Thanks a lot . . .' she said.

She'd snatched up her towel and got to her feet before I could take a breath. She seemed really angry for some reason.

'I'm going for a shower. And then I've got squash coaching.'

'Oh right . . .' I said.

'Do you think you can find your own way out?'

'Sure . . .'

I sat for a moment on the lounger thinking over what I'd said. I mean I was only giving her some friendly advice. She didn't have to take it so badly.

Within ten minutes or so she emerged from the women's changing rooms. She'd put on her squash gear.

She gave me a vague half-wave and with one last resentful glance, she flounced off. I watched those long legs make their way down the other side of the pool. Any *guy* but me might well have found her attractive.

At the door, she swung round and caught me watching her. With a glance that suggested just a flicker of triumph, she shot through it.

I lay back on the lounger and closed my eyes, trying to decide what to do next. I could hear the rain beating down on the glass roof of the swimming pool. Was the weather ever going to show any sign of clearing up?

I opened my eyes just a crack. Justine had left her sports holdall behind. It wasn't zipped up and on top of a pile of her things, with her customary carelessness, she'd left her house keys . . . Typical! I leaned over to do up the zip. But, come to think of it, they were, in actual fact . . . *my* keys!

My mind started racing. Friday . . . it was Mummy's Art School day. So the house would be empty. One hour's squash coaching should provide just enough time for a lightning dash to Cheyne Walk and a hunt for the Savings Certificate Book. After all, I reasoned, those savings were *my* money and I could always pay myself back . . .

The bus to Cheyne Walk kerb-crawled all the way up the King's Road. I think the driver was making up overtime or something. In the end I abandoned it and ran the last quarter mile. I reached Number 122, with my heart pounding in my chest and stood for a moment in the street staring up at the façade while I got my breath back.

The windows, between their baggy festoon blinds, peeped puffily back at me. Standing there, loitering with intent, I felt like a brand new, totally inexperienced burglar. All the 'Neighbourhood Watch' stickers on the neighbouring watching houses seemed turned, accusingly, on me.

I realized that the longer I stood there, the more criminal I looked. So with a quick glance to left and right, I strode up the front steps and turned the key in the lock.

Within a split second I was inside and had shut the front door with the professionalism of one who is apt to return a good half-hour after the negotiated curfew. Luckily, the burglar alarm had not gone off. Justine, with her usual slackness on security, had no doubt forgotten to set it when she left.

I stole up the stairs on tiptoe, and made for my room.

My room!

I closed the door gently and breathed in its familiar mixed aroma of Fendi, glossy magazines, dusting powder and – faint but distinguishable – my favourite old trainers.

My room! I checked it over. My eye came to rest on the dressing table. I don't believe it: Justine had dropped and shattered my Ultraglow – again!

I leaned over to try and salvage some of the bigger bits. Catching sight of the reflection in the mirror, I nearly hit the ceiling from shock. For a split second I hadn't recognized myself. I thought there was a *man* in my room!

I had to sit down on the bed for a minute to recover. This was totally *bi-zarre*!

Then, with tremendous strength of character, I pulled myself together and started the search for the Savings Book. Geesus, the drawers were in such a state! I couldn't have thrown anything away since I was six, practically.

I had just penetrated to the bottom of the third drawer of compacted birthday cards, Snoopy stationery sets and unfilled exercise books, when my progress was arrested by a sound . . .

I froze.

I could hear water running.

This could mean only one of two things. Either there was a freak high tide and the Thames Barrier had failed, or there was *someone in the house*.

I dived under the bed and lay there holding my breath.

The sound was coming from the room below. Mummy's bathroom. I put my ear to the floor and listened . . .

I could hear *Mummy's* voice saying something but it was kind of muffled and I couldn't tell what it was . . .

And then I heard another voice.

It was a male voice.

And it wasn't Daddy's.

After that there was a lot of *splashing*.

Now, I'm not in the least suspicious by nature. In fact, I would never have dreamed of suspecting *Mummy* of anything remotely extra-marital. Or even marital for that matter – she must be well-past-it, she's well over forty for godsake . . .

The splashing continued and I removed my stunned ear from the floor.

As a role model, clearly Mummy was getting totally out of line. Where would it all end? Frightful visions of the partition of 122, Cheyne Walk rose before my eyes. It was all too ghastly to contemplate. I could well need counselling for this . . .

That's when I caught sight of an old 'Penny Loafer' shoe box. Inside, surrounded by a gang of smelly rubbers and a load of fluff-encrusted discards from my sticker collection, was my long-lost National Savings Certificate Book.

Clasping hold of it, I slid out from under the bed. On silent feet, I abseiled down the stairwell.

I headed down the hall and closed the front door behind me.

I was still shaking from the tension of the whole thing as I reached the corner of Cheyne Walk and the second run of the day up to the King's Road didn't help one bit. By the time I reached the Number 22 bus stop I had decided that I definitely wasn't fitted for a life of crime. Some people simply can't take the stress.

I reached the Club at three minutes to one, charged across the grounds, zoomed into the Sports Complex, burst into the Pool Area, stuffed the keys back into Justine's bag and shot into the Men's Changing Room, just a split second before she emerged through the door, flushed and bright-eyed from her squash lesson.

I flattened myself against the tiled wall and observed her movements in the corner of a conveniently situated mirror. She picked up her holdall, looked around with a kind of lost-and-regretful expression, then moved out of my sightline. I could hear her squash shoes going squidge-squidge-squidge along the poolside. Then a door slammed and she had gone.

The coast was clear. I made my escape.

Twelve

It wasn't until I was practically back at Ferndale Avenue that I was struck by a minute, but crucial, flaw in my plan. Double-checking the number and value of my certificates – and I was right, I did have £100 worth – it occurred to me that although I could sign for the certificates with a clear conscience, I might look just that little bit suspect doing so. The Certificate Book said clearly – in indelible black ink – 'Justine Flora Duval (Miss)'.

Dire straits require drastic measures. Back at Number 45 there was, most fortuitously, no one at home. I penetrated into the sanctuary of Casper and Maggie's bedroom. Beyond their brass bed, spread with its handwoven Tibetan prayer rug, stood their wardrobe.

I rifled through a load of evening and ethnic wear trying to locate something vaguely wearable. Hang on, she actually had some original 'Seventies stuff – I was getting interested. A lot of this could most fruitfully be recycled as Grunge, man.

Once I had selected what seemed to be a passable armful of garments, I locked myself in the bathroom and started . . . the transformation.

Now Maggie, unfortunately, is rather on the small side. Each garment I put on, if anything, decreased my credibility as a female. The crutch of her tights came to somewhere just above my knees, the skirt zip wouldn't do up – and as to the sweater, even with Chuck's football scarf wound several times around my chest, it suggested a most unconvincing one-piece bust.

I studied my reflection critically. From above this fashion disaster area, a boy's face stared back at me. But it was nearly four o'clock. Two hours to go before the *Time Out* office closed . . .

Casting off any thoughts of aesthetics, I added a dash of Maggie's lipstick, a pair of dark glasses and a headscarf. Then, with a last bid for authenticity, I slipped a handbag over my arm and popped the Savings Certificate Book into it.

I successfully left the house before any of the Davises returned and hurried down the street towards Goldhawk Road Post Office. My speed was somewhat modified by the crutch of Maggie's tights which had by this time sunk to below my knees.

As a matter of fact, I caused quite a stir in the Post Office. People kind of coughed and stood aside for me and one small girl tugged at her mother's coat and, as she leaned down, whispered something in her ear.

So I reached the front of the queue in record time.

'Could I . . .' I adjusted my voice up an octave. 'I'd like to cash these, please.'

The desk clerk took my Savings Book and gave it a cursory glance, then, damping his fingers on his little orange Post Office sponge, he leaned over and reached into a drawer. But, *stress-factor*, instead of counting out nice crisp £10 notes, he shoved my book, a form and a manilla envelope under the grille.

'What's this for?'

'Just fill out the form and send it in,' he said.

I couldn't be hearing this.

'You mean, I don't get the money right away?'

127

'You have to send in for it. They've got to work out the interest, you see.'

'Don't worry about the interest. Keep it. I just want my money now.'

The Post Office clerk stared at me as if I'd offered him a bribe or something.

'Look, Miss . . .' he said. 'There are people behind you and they all want to get served before the end of the day. Savings Certificates have to be dealt with at Head Office.'

'But how long will it take?' I asked.

'The money should be with you within eight days . . .'

(*Eight days!*)

'Next,' he said firmly. And the woman with the small girl moved up to the counter, giving me a wide berth.

Dejectedly, I made my way back to 45, Ferndale Avenue. As I reached the house I realized three things. The 2CV was standing outside which meant Maggie was back. Chuck's light was on which meant Chuck was back. And it had stopped raining!

I retrieved my bucket and squeegee from under the hedge, about-turned and headed back down the road.

You can have no idea of the novelty value of a windscreen washer in drag. Reactions varied from overtly sexist wolf-whistles to offers of all sorts of things in the back seat. I have never felt so humiliated in my whole life.

I had had just about enough of being jeered at and was going to chuck it in when these guys hauled into sight pushing a bath on wheels. The bath was full of water and had a mermaid in it. No seriously! After them came a whole load of people dressed as clowns and the front and back ends of horses and things. And they were all shaking buckets like mine.

It just so happened, with the kind of fortuitous timing that crosses the average human being's path about twice a century like Halley's comet, that a Rag Parade from the local Hospital was passing by.

I couldn't have fitted in better if I'd purposely dressed for the part, so I kind of fell in line with them and shook my bucket along with the others.

Before I knew it, my bucket was filling up nicely. I guess not many of the people who gave me money realized that the Rag I was collecting for was *Time Out* – but honestly, I swear here and now, this was purely a loan. I solemnly promise that the minute those Savings Certificates are cashed, I'll hotfoot it along to the Hospital and put every penny back into their New Wing Appeal.

By five o'clock, I had ducked out of the procession and was counting my takings. I had well over £25, so enough for the ad and my tube fare to the *Time Out* offices in Southampton Street and back.

Predictably, there was a hold-up on the Northern Line. I stood wedged between early commuters and late shoppers, steaming with rage and Northern Line body-heat. Just as I had given up all hope of making it in time, the train started up again with a jolt and a wheeze and I reached the *Time Out* Offices just as all the clocks in the City were striking six o'clock. The staff were filing out of the main doors as I forced my way in against the flow.

I don't think *Time Out* Classifieds are used to straight cash deals. Frankly, the girl who took the money seemed a little stunned. But she accepted the bucketful, all the same. As she counted out the last pennies, I heaved a huge sigh of relief.

So now all I had to do was to sit back and wait for the ad to work. Simple, really!

★

I felt pretty euphoric when I left the *Time Out* Office. In fact, I headed straight for the nearest pub and asked for the telephone. I had to let Chuck know right away.

I lifted the receiver and dialled the number.

'Hello?'

It was Maggie.

'Hi, it's me . . . Jake. Is Chuck there?'

'No, he's not. Will you be back for supper? Chuck wasn't sure?'

'Yes . . . I mean . . . I think so. Please.'

(How on earth was I going to make an appearance dressed like this?)

'It'll be on the table at eight, then,' said Maggie. 'Oh and by the way – Air India rang.'

'Really?'

'Bad news about the luggage, I'm afraid. You're going to have to claim on their insurance. I'll explain later.'

'Oh dear.'

'Don't be late.'

'No . . . I mean, right,' I said. 'Thanks. See you then!'

I rang off thoughtfully. Where was Chuck? Hang on, maybe he was at Justine's.

I dialled her number.

She must have been virtually sitting on the phone.

'Hi Justine.'

'Hi,' I could tell by her voice she'd recognized mine. She was still sounding kind of cold and resentful.

'Look, is Chuck with you?'

'No, why?'

'Just wondered, he's not at home.'

There was a meaningful pause. She was quite obviously waiting for me to make some amends for our last memorable conversation.

'Well, I just rang to say . . . about this morning – I think perhaps I might have upset you in some way?'

'Hold on a minute. I'll take this upstairs. Bit more privacy.'

Privacy! What did she think I was going to do? Start heavy breathing?

I dropped another 20p in the slot.

'Who's eavesdropping?' I asked when she came back on the line.

'Mummy, she gets some sort of vicarious thrill from listening in. She has such a dull life, poor dear.'

Evidently she had no inkling that Mummy was playing the *femme fatale*. Maybe this was the key moment I'd been waiting for to enlighten her.

'She's at a dangerous age . . .' I started.

'What were you saying about this morning?'

'Well you seemed a bit pee-ed off, that's all.'

'Forget it . . .' she said. 'Guess I was just in a bit of a mood. Was that all you wanted . . .?'

'Do you think she can still hear us?'

'Who?'

'Your mother.'

'No . . . I don't think so.'

'What's she been doing all day?'

'I've no idea . . . why?'

'Well, women, you know, she's at a tricky age – mid-fortyish, wondering what she's missed.'

'What do you mean?'

'Well, they can tend to indulge in *extra-curricula activities*!'

'Don't tell me,' said Justine, resolutely not taking the hint. 'She's actually talked about joining the Open University. These days, she barely has time to restock the fridge. I can't understand it, she never had any interests before.'

'Interests?' I prompted with feigned innocence. Actually, the thought of Mummy's solid and reliable form, stripped of her colour-coordinated Jaeger separates, suddenly made the whole thing seem so terribly improbable.

'Oh she's into art in a big way. She's spent an absolute

fortune in Green and Stone and bought herself a wheelie-easel and a gross kind of striped smock thing to paint in. It's all rather gone to her head. She's just chucked in painting classes because she thinks she knows it all.'

'Really?' (That explained why she was at home this morning . . . partly . . .)

'Umm. She's actually got a commission for a portrait. Had her first sitting today. An Afghan.'

An exotic vision of Mummy with this robed and turbaned sitter leaped to mind.

'Arrived absolutely filthy apparently,' Justine continued. 'She had to insist he had a bath before she could lift a paintbrush. You should have seen the state of her bathroom.'

All that splashing. Chelsea hadn't sunk to such depths of bohemianism since the days of Augustus John.

'Hey Jake . . . you still there?'

'Yes . . . but I can't talk for long.'

A guy had just come out of the Gents; kind of hitching up his trousers and scratching, he hovered by the phone. His face was somehow familiar.

Oh my god, it wasn't. Yes it was. It was Bum-Cleave.

''Ello darlin',' he said with a leer.

I adjusted my voice.

'Got to go,' I shrilled.

'Jake . . . you OK?'

I left the pub in record time and made for the tube.

(Actually, it was Maggie who put me straight about Mummy in the end. She told me some time later, in a kind of condescending tone which I thought was quite uncalled-for, that Mummy had found her true vocation as an artist — in Dog Portraits.)

Anyway after a most agonizing half-hour strap-hanging in the rush-hour crush, during which time my bust descended to waist-level no less than three times, I made it to Earl's Court. After several false starts, I located a phone that worked.

'Hey Chuck, is that you?'

'Where are you?'

'Earls Court station.'

'So you didn't get the money?' he said in a cold flat tone.

'Yes I did, *and* I got it to *Time Out* in time – just.'

'Well. Guess you can come back here then.'

'Bit difficult . . .'

'What's the problem?'

'Clothing mainly.'

'What do you mean?'

'If you could head over here with my jeans and sweatshirt – I think they're somewhere on the bathroom floor – I'll love you forever.'

There was a pause while Chuck ascertained their exact location.

'You standing there starkers or something?'

'Not exactly.'

'What d'you mean – not exactly?'

'You'll see . . .' I said and rang off.

'Geesus,' said Chuck when he saw me. 'Oh my God . . .' and he cracked up.

He was still killing himself when I emerged, rather speedily, from the Ladies, back in my own jeans and sweatshirt. He held the doors of the Richmond train open for me which was handy because I had this large West Indian lady asserting her authority as Official Loo Attendant, in hot pursuit. I don't think she took too kindly to people having a quick sex change in her 'Convenience'.

After the exertions of the past eight hours, I was hoping for praise or, at the very least, sympathy. But Chuck just sat in his seat shaking with silent laughter. Frankly, I didn't see what was so wildly funny. I had had a very long, very difficult day. However, the laughter had one good effect, it kind of healed the rift between us, so grudgingly I joined in.

'Oh, by the way,' said Chuck, pulling himself together with an effort and trying to wipe the smirk from his face. 'Justine rang. She wants me to meet up with her tonight.' He looked rather pleased with himself.

'Just you?'

'Yes, just me. Why?'

'Just wondered.'

(I was thinking, rather uncharitably, that the reason for this sudden invitaion might have something to do with the fact that Alex was being let out of hospital today.)

Actually Chuck's triumph didn't last that long. When we got back Maggie had a message from Justine – to the effect, 'Why didn't Chuck bring Jake along too?'

But I wasn't going to spoil his rare moment of triumph. Actually, I had better things in mind. I was looking forward to a pleasant evening doing absolutely F-all.

Maggie and Casper were going to see some obscure black and white movie with subtitles, so I was planning a night nicely vegging out slug-fashion in front of the TV, zapping through some decent trash.

'Why don't you invite Alex?' I suggested innocently to Chuck.

'Do me a favour,' he said.

As it happened, it took quite a time to get Chuck out of the house. He kept changing his mind about what he was going to wear.

I had dimmed the lights, taken possession of the sofa and didn't intend to move more than the muscle in my remote control finger for the rest of the evening.

Chuck kept appearing in the sitting room doorway.

'Do you think it would be better if I went casual – the Aran sweater look?'

I shrugged.

'What about my black Levi's and leather jacket?'

'Up to you . . .'

He disappeared upstairs and I could hear him ransacking Casper's chest of drawers.

He reappeared wearing Casper's gross Icelandic handknit. 'What do you think?'

'Do you want me to be kind, or to be honest?'

'Look, could you give me some idea. You should know what she likes for godsake. Should I or shouldn't I shave?'

'She likes you as you are.'

I hadn't the heart to tell him that even if he had major plastic surgery, an intensive body-building course, and umpteen deep-tanning sessions, he wouldn't stand a chance with Justine. No, it was perfectly clear who she had her cool heart set on. I should know for godsake. I'd been keen on Alex practically forever . . . well, for two months at any rate.

In the end Chuck was ready to leave – almost noticeably unshaven, his hair gelled back so it unfortunately looked as if it was prematurely receding, and positively soaked in Xeros.

'This OK?' he said, pausing in the doorway.

'If she passes out from the aftershave, don't take advantage of her, that's all,' I said.

'No worries, I'm prepared,' he said patting his pocket.

I zapped to another channel.

Then it suddenly occurred to me what he meant. I zoomed out of the front door and down the front path but by the time I reached the gate he had rounded the corner and was out of sight.

'Oh well, dream on,' I thought. He didn't stand a chance anyway.

Actually, as luck would have it, none of the trash was worth zapping-to that night. Out of sheer desperation, I started sorting through the Davis' collection of videos. They seemed to have recorded most of *Panorama* and *The World About Us*, nothing remotely erotic apart from a load of rhinos and fruitflies and things doing it. At last, I came across an unreturned video-shop cassette. It was the *Nightmare on Elm Street* I'd lost yonks ago and Daddy had had to pay up for.

I settled down to watch it . . .

Half an hour later I was well into wishing that I'd lost something rather less scary. I put the video on Pause, crept into the kitchen, found Stalin, and carried him back to the sofa for company.

We had just come to the bit in the bath which always totally freaks me out when Stalin went completely rigid. I mean, I never realized cats watched television with that much attention . . .

And then I heard it.

It wasn't the television Stalin was reacting to . . .

It was a noise coming from the back of the house. An irregular knocking noise followed by an eerie kind of dragging sound.

I turned the TV sound down and froze. The noise was getting nearer. Stalin, electrified, leaped off my lap and darted under the sofa.

Tap . . . tap . . . tap . . . draaaaggg . . . went the noise.

It was followed by a chilling knocking on the French windows and a 'Hi, anyone at home?'

It was Alex's voice. His face appeared framed between the leaded panes.

'God,' I said. 'Am I glad to see you!'

'That's nice,' said Alex, as I let him in. He propped his crutches up against the wall and eased himself into a chair. His leg was in plaster up to to the knee and he had a funny kind of sock-shoe thing over the toe.

'Anyone else at home? Any beer in the fridge?'

I fetched some beers and by the time we were on to our third I was starting to feel less shaky. Actually, Alex really was looking rather divine. He was wearing his well-faded Levi's shirt and a kind of soft suede jacket the colour of naked sun-bronzed skin. One of the legs of his perfectly worn-out 501s had been ripped off at the knee to allow for the plaster cast. The knee that protruded was muscular, golden and evenly flecked with hairs that just caught the light. . . .

Here we were *alone together*, for the very *first time* in our *lives*. The *lights* were *low*, the sofa *beckoned* and there was a really scary movie on hand to provide a legitimate excuse for sitting *seductively close*.

But just when it mattered most my sexual status put the whole thing on *ice*. Oh how could life be *soo-oo* . . . *unfair*?

He was being really matey.

'So where's Chuck?'

'Out with Justine.'

Alex raised an eyebrow. 'Really?'

'Yep, he made a real effort – didn't shave, gelled his hair, the works . . .'

Alex leaned back in his chair.

'He should be OK then. She's a real little go-er,' he said.

'Pardon?' I said. I didn't think I could have heard right.

'Yep!' said Alex. 'Can't get enough of it. You know how her school and our school met up last Easter on that Biology Field Trip?'

'Ye-es . . .' I said.

'Oh boy. What an afternoon that was!'

'Tell me about it?' (*I was simply dying to hear.*)

'Well, it just so happened that Justine and I were teamed up studying the limpet population on the Upper Shore of Folkestone Bay. You'll never guess what happened? . . .'

(*Wanna-bet? I was there for godsake.*)

'No idea,' I prompted. I was all ears.

'Got any more beer?'

I passed him a bottle.

Alex took a swig and wiping his mouth on the back of his hand he leaned forward.

'Personally, I put a lot of it down to the limpets.' He licked his lips: 'Dead sexy you know, limpets.'

'Really?'

'Well, just think for a moment – there they are clamped to the rock with the next limpet maybe fifteen to twenty millimetres away – how do you think they *do* it?'

'Very rarely, I should think . . .'

'Nah, they're at it all the time. Did you know that, scaled up to human proportions, the dick of the average limpet is roughly equivalent to the length of Nelson's column?'

I tried to look impressed. Actually, this wasn't news to me. I'd got an 'A' for my Folkestone Limpet Project.

'So what happened with Justine?' I asked.

(*Aren't we simply dying to know?*)

'Well, it started with a pretty thorough snog . . . real tongue-in stuff . . . you know . . .'

(*A Gross Untruth! We never got out of the sightline of Mr Blenkinsop's theodolite.*)

'Then she simply went wild, ripping the clothes off me. Boy, what a session that was . . .'

'Memorable, was it?' I asked drily.

'I should say so . . . What a go-er . . .!' He took another contemplative swig of his beer.

(I was seething. I practically had steam coming out of my ears. How could anyone have the nerve to come out with such complete and utter bare-faced lies!)

'Still keeping this *thing* going with her, *are you*?' I enquired, trying to control my voice.

'Nah . . . not really, you know – females – they tend to think they own your body if you give them too much security. Best to keep the options open . . .'

Alex then went into a long list of the other females who had enjoyed the thrill of brief moments of his undivided attention.

'Must hold you back a bit having that on . . .' I said pointing at his plaster cast.

'Yeah, well, gives a guy a chance to recharge, I guess,' he said.

'Know what . . . you should liven that leg up a bit. Get all the fans to sign it.'

'Sure. Why not. Good idea,' said Alex.

'I'll go and find a pen.'

I went into the kitchen and selected Maggie's thick black indelible linen marker from the dresser drawer.

'Hold still now,' I said.

Alex obediently sat with his leg outstretched, supported by the footstool.

'No peeping.'

In very large indelible letters I wrote across the front of his plaster cast:

Alex Marchant is a Wanker

'That should do.'

'Can I look now?'

After that Alex made a pretty concerted effort to thump me – a tricky manoeuvre on crutches. He was still thrashing around swearing and knocking things over when Chuck arrived back.

'Hey, hold it. What's going on?' said Chuck, switching on the main light.

'Geesus,' said Alex. 'Look what the bastard's done to me!'

Chuck looked. The little smile lines around his mouth twitched, and then he frowned.

'Why did you do that, Jake?'

'Alex was saying uncalled-for things about a certain female we know.' I raised an eyebrow.

'Franz?'

'Close.'

'Henry?'

'Closer.'

'Not Justine?'

'I only said that she was a bit of a go-er. What's wrong with that?'

'A go-er did you say?' said Chuck exchanging glances with me.

'A bit of a go-er,' corrected Alex.

'A *bit* of a go-er. Doesn't sound wildly exciting to me. Does it to you Jake?'

I shook my head. 'Apparently it all happened on that Biology Field Trip last year. You were there, weren't you? Did you notice Justine *go*-ing for Alex at all?'

'Not a lot,' said Chuck. 'But then I never really rated Justine much as a go-er.'

'You just don't know how to turn her on, mate,' said Alex, recovering some of his assertiveness.

'How do you mean?' said Chuck.

'Handle her right and she comes on red hot . . .'

(*He made me sound like some kind of faulty plumbing.*)

'She speaks very well of you too . . .' said Chuck.

'Oh yeah. So what does she think of me then?' asked Alex settling into his chair again and preparing to have his ego stroked.

Chuck glanced down at Alex's plaster cast and we both cracked up.

Alex went home in disgust after that.

He only lived two doors down from Chuck. A fact which,

I guess, solves the mystery of why they were 'such good mates'. Chuck's was his closest outlet for constant 'fixes' of beer and bragging.

Thirteen

'So how did it go with Justine?' I asked when we were stacked in our bunks.

'Fine,' said Chuck. He was being very non-commital.

'Come on. I've a right to know. Did you try to get off with her?'

'Not exactly.'

'So what did you do?'

'Talked mainly. About Alex to start with. Oh, by the way . . . I found out why Franz thinks Alex is a prat.'

(Now this was more like gossip, man). I leaned over.

'Well you know how last Friday Franz invited Alex round for a meal?'

'Uh huh?'

'Apparently, she'd gone to a lot of trouble. Her parents were scheduled to be out till two or something so she knew they'd have the house to themselves . . . Her mother had left them something really passion-killing like shepherd's pie. But she'd dumped it down the waste-disposal and made a real effort – she'd bought candles and everything – raided the deep-freeze – three whole courses from M&S – the works.'

'Yeah?'

'Well Alex turned up and he saw the table laid out like an open invitation – with the bottle of wine and even flowers and stuff, and he suddenly suggested they went out and made-a-night-of-it.'

'Sounds a bit out of character to me.'

'You wait . . . gets better. First of all Franz was really flattered.' Chuck raised an eyebrow. 'Dinner out, we all know what that means.'

'Sure.'

'It was a bit on the early side, so he suggested they took in a film first. He made Franz sit through something she'd seen before – *and* she paid for herself. Afterwards he said, "So let's grab something to eat". Well, they were walking up the King's Road and Franz was getting all ready for the sweet-lights-and-soft-music treatment when he suddenly lurched off into McDonald's.'

'You're kidding!'

'Nope. He ate two Big Macs and – according to Justine's version – belched. Then he put on his Horny-as-Alex expression, stretched, flexing all his muscles, and said, "I'm really tired".'

'Uh huh?'

'Well, naturally Franz thought – this is "it"! She whipped him out on to the street and whistled down a taxi.'

'Are we coming to the interesting bit now?'

'Yep . . . Alex opened the door for her like a real gent. She climbed in. He closed the door and leaned through the window and said, "See you then, must dash, that's my bus".'

'Was that "it"?'

'Yep. Not so much as a mini-snog-ette.'

'Geesus,' I said and lay back looking at the ceiling. 'Not exactly date-rape, was it?' Then I had a good smirk to myself. (Men! . . . *MEN*!!).

'So you didn't have a whole load to live up to with Justine then?' I said trying to control my voice and sound 'concerned-and-interested'.

'Not exactly . . .'

'Well?'

'I think maybe she was a bit overcome by having the full force of my undivided attention,' Chuck said thoughtfully.

'In other words, it might have been better if I'd gone too?'

'You could say that. You might as well have been there, actually.'

'What do you mean?'

'She spent the entire "rest-of-the-whole-damn-evening" talking about *you*.'

'Oh, you're not starting on that again.'

'I'm telling you – she's got the hots for you.'

'Rubbish!'

'And I'll tell you another thing, I reckon so has Franz.'

In a totally bizarre way, I felt rather flattered.

'Come off it. Don't be ridiculous. What makes you think that? I'm hardly Franz's type.'

'I'm doing my best to put her off.'

'How?'

'I told her you were a bit of an intellectual.'

'That should do the trick.'

'Not according to Justine. Apparently Franz has taken to spending hours holed up in her room with the collected works of Wittgenstein.'

Now the nearest I had ever known Franz get to a serious solitary activity was plucking all the hairs out her legs one by one with eyebrow tweezers. Chuck was starting to get me worried.

'Anyway,' he continued. 'Whether you believe me or not, I'm warning you: don't give either of those girls the slightest bit of encouragement or they'll try and move in.'

With those ominous words, Chuck turned over in his bunk and totally callously went to sleep.

I lay in the top bunk wide awake trying to get my mind

around what I'd actually learned about the male of the species. Life was so much simpler for a girl! I thought of myself back in those happier days tucked up in my Cheyne Walk bed innocently dreaming of Dangerous Liaisons with what had turned out to be a Prize Wanker.

I guess I could forgive Alex for being an ego-tripper . . . a bit of male arrogance is OK – adds to the attraction if anything. I could even overlook the fact he was a total chauvinist pig . . . most men are.

But what I really couldn't forgive was all this 'Kiss and Tell' business. No, hang on – correction! It was worse – it was 'Not-Kissing and Telling' that I couldn't forgive. Boasting about first degree passion in the sand dunes when he hadn't even had the decency to lay a finger on me! God what a RAT!

Alex Marchant! – there he was touting himself around as a Worldly Wise Womaniser, when he was nothing of the sort! Just to think that I had actually believed he was drop dead gorgeous – the guy who was going to initiate me into all the illicit bliss of a *real relationship* and the fact was, he was – all TALK! – just as immature and inept – just as totally useless as guys like Chuck. Geesus – the disillusionment!

Next morning, I was once again subjected to the harsh realities of street life. After my encounter with the Earl's Court Road 'cartel' I had decided to resite my business enterprise in what estate agents call 'a more prestigious location'. My new pitch was at the top of Sloane Street, just outside Harvey Nix.

I worked through the morning in a kind of half-daze. I was becoming *au fait* with the finer points of the profession. I could spot a single-sweep wiper half a mile off – like Citroen CXs (they also have concave rear windows which are positive dirt traps), so their drivers are often good for 50p.

Porsche 924 and 944 drivers simply adore being asked if they'd like their headlamps done – just to show off the coy way the lights pop up, like the eyes on Walt Disney turtles.

Actually, it was a pretty good day for business. By mid-morning I switched over from the Knightsbridge station side to give my other squeegee arm a turn.

I was lost in concentrated thought about something of deep windscreen-washing significance, trying out a brand new squeegee action on this pretty straightforward Volvo . . . when I noticed there was something familiar about the licence holder. As I made a sweep of the screen in a single deft movement, I . . .

. . . leapt back as if I'd come face to face with a cobra.

It was . . . *Mummy*!

And there, sitting beside her, was Justine. She was dressed in immaculate jodhpurs and her hacking jacket. Evidently on her way back from a revitalizing morning ride in the Row.

'Jake . . .' gasped Justine. 'What are you doing here?'

'Do you know this person?' demanded Mummy, who was scrabbling in her purse.

'Yes . . . he's a . . . friend of Chuck's,' stammered Justine.

'I see,' said Mummy. She swapped the 10p she was going to give me for a 50p.

'Here you are, young man,' she said. 'Nice to meet you.' And she zoomed up her window, crashed into gear, and drove off at some speed.

I went back to window-washing convinced that I had sunk well below the bottom line of social acceptability.

However, it seems that I had grossly underestimated the social tolerance of this particular female. Within half an hour, a swift, determined figure in jodhpurs emerged from

Knightsbridge tube station and strode across the road towards me.

'Hi!' said Justine.

'Hi!' I replied and continued washing the Peugeot estate I was dealing with at the time.

'Look, I've got to talk to you.'

The chap in the Peugeot called out: 'Oi . . .. Do you think you could finish my windscreen first?'

I whipped around the car to do the other side.

'Can you stop that and listen?' shouted Justine.

'Sorry, I'm with a client at the moment. Could you call back later?'

'Oh look, Jake, be serious!'

I continued squeegee-ing like a maniac.

Justine walked round to the front of the Peugeot and stood in the road, barring the way so that the car couldn't go forward without running her over.

'I'm not moving until you listen to me.'

The driver handed me a 20p and added his point of view. Several cars behind his joined in, hooting with determination, and a taxi driver shouted something unprintable.

'OK,' I said. 'You win.'

I staked my claim to this prime location by positioning my bucket and squeegee in a key vantage point by the traffic lights, and allowed Justine to escort me into Joe's Café.

Blandly ignoring the black looks from the waiter, Justine sat me down at a table and ordered two large cappuccinos.

'Look,' she said. 'What precisely is going on?'

I mumbled something about needing some ready money.

'But I thought you had this really big business thing going?'

'Well, I might have exaggerated the scale of things a bit,' I said, playing with my spoon, sorting through the little coloured sugar crystals.

'Tell me the truth! Are you wildly in debt?' she demanded.

I had to admit I had a loan to repay.

'What's it for?'

'The West Wing of the Kensington and Chelsea Hospital.'
Justine's eyes widened.

'It must be vast!'

I shrugged, 'These things are relative.'

'Oh poor you . . .' she paused . . . 'But windscreen washing! To sink to that! Maybe Daddy can help.'

'Oh, I wouldn't want to . . .'

'I've got it!' she said. 'You can work for Jason.'

'Who's Jason?' I asked innocently.

'Franz's half-brother. He's opening a nightclub. He's
bound to need help.'

(Now, just to fill you in, Jason is part of the upper-crust
underworld – made most of his money running raves –
he's staggeringly wealthy for a 20-year-old, has £50 notes
positively oozing out of his back pockets – but – he's also,
unfortunately, tight as hell with it. Justine had evidently
defied 'Mummy' and re-established contact with Jason and
Co – otherwise known in our circle as 'The Mafia' but
whom Mummy always referred to as 'those dreadful people'.)

I was only halfway through my cappuccino but Justine
practically dragged me out of Joe's and flagged down a taxi.

'Where are we going?' I asked, feigning ignorance.

'Victoria. He should be at the Club by now. We'll try and
catch him before he gets snowed under.'

Some minutes later our taxi came to a halt outside what
looked very much like the site of some major disaster.

It was over a week now since I'd last passed the Club and
by all appearances the only thing had been done was that a
load of slightly wonky letters had been screwed up to the
fascia which read 'BUCKINGHAM PALACE' and, underneath, 'SW1's most exclusive venue'.

Beneath this there was a mountain of scaffolding and signs

that said things like: 'You are entering a hard hat area'. And 'Beware. Guard dogs on patrol'.

A load of workmen were running a sort of chain gang balanced on planks passing buckets of rubble and cement back and forth.

'This way . . .' said Justine and disappeared down the run of planks into the gloom.

I groped my way after her. I'd been dying to see what it was like inside.

Inside it was icy cold and pitch-dark and underfoot it had the feel of rotting carpet over gently decaying dogs.

'It looks like there's a hell of a lot to be done,' I said.

'I know and they're opening on Monday,' said Justine.

'Monday! You can't be serious.'

'Franz says Jason needs all the help he can get.'

She disappeared from sight through a set of mahogany doors.

'Where are you?' her voice called back to me, echoing as if she had reached a very large cave.

'Wicked, isn't it?' she said when I found her. 'You'll be able to see more when they get electricity of course.'

We were standing in a vast panelled ballroom. As my eyes adjusted to the gloom I made out a kind of ghostly gothic splendour, all scratched mahogany and pitted mirrors amply festooned with spiderwebs and dusty plush.

Justine led the way through a forest of upturned chairs. I followed, gingerly groping my way between long fingers of tattered velvet.

There was a very large reproduction portrait of the Queen propped up against one wall. The Queen was gazing disapprovingly at a load of pink-plaster naked ladies having what looked like an orgy in the corner. Beside them there was a stuffed iguana in a glass case.

'That's the decor,' said Justine and disappeared up a spiral staircase.

At the top of this, after negotiating a labyrinth of inky corridors, we came across a door with a yellow 'Post-it' slip stuck on it that said 'Office'.

Justine threw open the door and beckoned to me.

'Meet Jason,' she said.

A figure in the gloom was making signals to us to keep quiet. He continued with his phone conversation.

'OK, so I guess it's final. We'll just have to reprint.'

He put the phone down, greased over to us and gave Justine a pat on the bottom.

'Hi, Gorgeous,' he said. 'Who did you say this was?'

'Jake . . . he wants to help.'

'Cool . . .!' said Jason. 'Follow me!'

'By the way, we've got to think of a new name,' he continued over his shoulder as he went bounding down the spiral staircase. '*Someone*'s complained.'

We scrambled after him.

'What a drag . . .!' said Justine.

'TeaBag!' he shouted.

The sound of a distant voice came from somewhere up near the ceiling, 'Hang on . . . be right with you . . .'

Suddenly the laser lights came on. We stood there, all mottled with whirling spots as if we'd come out in mobile measles.

'How's that?' came the voice from above.

'Fantastic!'

A figure sailed down a vertical ladder barely touching the rungs and bounced to a halt in front of us.

'Hello there!' TeaBag was massive. His hair was mainly shaven round the sides leaving a kind of flat plateau of tight black curls on top. He grinned as he looked around, admiring the effect of the lights.

'Yo! That's what I call a light show, man! All we need to fix now is the music. And we can partyyyy!'

'OK TeaBag, back to work. We've got to get the guys to take the name down from outside.'

'But we only just put it up!'

'Don't argue! Do it!' said Jason and hurled himself back up the stairs.

TeaBag whistled through his teeth and headed for the front of the building.

'So what can I do?' I said, casting round at the chaos wondering where to begin.

At that moment Jason's voice was heard yelling down the stairwell.

'Justine! Phone!'

I followed her and watched as she picked up the receiver.

'Hi! How did you guess I was here?'

(It's Franz, she mouthed at me.)

'He's here with me. . . . What?. . . . Oh God, no . . . completely forgot . . . cancellation charge? . . . really? . . . how much? . . . Geesus! All right! If I must. Yes, *all right*! I'm leaving now!'

'God!' she said, slamming the phone down. 'Now I've got to go. Franz has booked me in for this really tedious all-day session with her at the Sanctuary. It'd completely slipped my mind.'

So Justine left for a 'really tedious' day of body-pampering in the warm perfumed cocoon of the Sanctuary. And I was left in the dank, dark, freezing cold with Franz's manic half-brother on my hands.

I was given the job of manning the phones and telling everyone that Jason wasn't there, particularly if they wanted anything that sounded like money.

There were loads of calls from people who thought they should be paid for boring things like plasterboard and insulated cabling and double-thickness polystyrene soundproofing. Then there were slightly more interesting calls from hangers-on who were supplying the Club with things like backgammon boards and one-armed bandits and Japanese finger buffets. There was one lovely lady who said she was making a nine-foot diameter cake and wanted to know if we wanted royal or piped icing on it. There was a terribly tired girl called Camilla from *Tatler* who was enquiring whether the case of Moët et Chandon had arrived for the crew on the opening night and could I be a poppet and see that it was put on ice. And in between all of these there were constant calls from a wild Italian who kept asking for a Mr Gladstone and wouldn't take no for an answer when I said there was no one of that name about.

I soon found asking the callers to hang on made them really go ape-s***. So instead I decided to adopt this kind of electronic voice which said, 'Sorry caller you are in a queuing system, your call will be answered in strict rotation' – and then cut them off.

Yonks later when I had answered and cut off most of the suppliers of the London social scenery, Jason asked me if I would like to do something else for a change.

I don't want to bore you with an account of the entire day. Enough to say that my effective job title went something like: phone-answerer-coffee-carrier-TeaBag-finder-loo-roll-swopper-floor-swabber-mirror-polisher-black-rubbish-bag-dumper.

Still, I guess that's the nightclub business. Actually, I thought I did pretty well. It isn't everyone who can handle the pace and the glamour.

Fourteen

I arrived home that night very late indeed, to find a note to the effect that a chickpea stew had been left to congeal in the Aga for me and that everyone had gone to bed.

Having consumed the less rock-hard bits of the meal, I crawled upstairs and climbed into the top bunk.

Jason, TeaBag and I had ended the day by disconnecting the phones and had spent a fruitless evening wrestling with the task of finding a new name for the Club. Eventually, when we'd filled his office with smoke, despondency, and polystyrene coffee cups full of chewed gum and fag ends, Jason had said, 'Let's sleep on it.'

Easier said than done. Whether it was from the inflationary effect of the chickpeas or the taunting sound of Chuck's steady breathing coming up from below – I could find no way of making myself comfortable.

Eventually my manic stirring must have woken Chuck.

'Having a party up there?'

'No listen, I can't sleep.'

'So I gathered; what's the problem?'

'I've got to find a new name for a nightclub by the morning.'

'How about "Insomnia",' suggested Chuck.

'Very funny.'

'Try counting dodos.'

I tried. Every time I was about to drop off, I was awoken by the sound of Chuck turning over or punching his pillow or something.

'What's the matter?'

'Now I can't sleep either!'

Chuck switched the light on and located a piece of paper and a Biro.

'Let's get this sorted,' he said.

We soon had built up quite a list. Then we worked down it eliminating anything that was too obvious, or too obscure.

'How many have we got left?'

'Two', said Chuck. 'But I've a feeling they've been done before.'

I looked over his shoulder.

'Maybe "Insomnia" wasn't such a bad idea after all.'

'What we need is expert advice,' said Chuck.

He opened the bedroom door and reached for the phone.

'You can't call people at this hour.'

'They should just about be getting home. It's three-thirty,' said Chuck.

His call was answered.

'Yeah, hardcore. In need of your wriggly grey. Gotta tag a venue.' I didn't need to be told who Chuck had called.

'......'

'Matt wants to know what kind of crowd . . .?' Chuck said as an aside to me.

I gave him a brief run-down. Chuck translated.

'No casuals, no raggas, no psychedelies – hopefully a mix of true poseurs and real buttery grungies, mainpart 16 to 25.'

'......'

'Location off-centre – West-Central, sounds a real weird-scene venue, like gothic man.'

'......'

After that a whole list of words was dictated down the line like machine gun fire. It was as much as Chuck could do to get them all down.

When he'd rung off, we studied the result.

Virtually every word began with E, or had Ecstatic connotations. Chuck shook his head.

'Trouble with those guys, they're one-trackers. Come on, the two of us can crack this. What's the real crux of this venue?'

I shrugged, 'Its size I guess.'

Chuck chewed at the end of his Bic.

'Like how big?'

I struggled for a comparison.

'Kind of a cross between the Palais and the Hippodrome.'

'So when's it opening?'

'On Monday . . .'

Chuck flicked through his diary.

'Four-nine-ninety-four – it's a palindrome,' he said.

Then he repeated:

'*The Palindrome*!' with such explosive conviction that the little plastic bit from the top of his Biro hit the ceiling. 'That's it!'

'The Palindrome . . .?' I echoed doubtfully.

'Yeah!' said Chuck and he was scribbling on his piece of paper again.

'What are you doing?'

'Designing the flyers. . . .'

Next day I took Chuck's rough scribbles into the office with me.

THE PALINDROME
Grand opening 4/9/94

Featuring: And
LIVE EVIL   STAR RATS
Dress code: Anything reversible

Nostalgia spot: AႡBA

By ten o'clock Jason still hadn't turned up so I left the piece of paper in a prominent place on his desk and went to get a coffee from the café round the corner.

By the time I got back Jason had arrived but the piece of paper had mysteriously disappeared. We couldn't find TeaBag either.

He was gone for quite some time.

He'd been at the CopyShop. He had taken Chuck's scribbles with him. They'd printed 10,000 flyers. So the name kind of stuck.

Jason was livid about it. But, in actual fact, he hadn't come up with an alternative. While he ranted and raved about it, TeaBag was busy organizing the crew into putting up a whole new set of letters on the front of the building.

'PALINDROME' read Jason, backing across Victoria Street with his hands in his pockets to study the effect of the new sign, and scattering a drove of Number 19 buses as he did so.

'Well, I guess I'll have to try and live with it,' he said grudgingly.

By three that afternoon the flyers had begun to circulate through the vast network of London subterranean subculture and the office phones were in constant ring mode.

I was coming into my own as a telephone answering service', 'The Palindrome – how can I help you? Yes, opening on Monday. No comps, I'm afraid. How many do you want ...? No credit cards, just give me your name and you can pay cash on the door.'

156

Jason was leaning back in his chair with his feet on his desk accepting phoned congratulations for the brilliant concept and totting up on his calculator how much he was likely to make on the first night.

Actually, apart from pleasing Jason, who was getting all the credit, it was handy having the name up because the numerous assorted commercial vehicles that had been searching London for the last twenty-four hours, trying to track down the actual location of the Club, now had something to home in on. Quite suddenly, they all descended on the place en masse.

At around four o'clock I staggered out of the office, shell-shocked from a stint on the phones, to find the dance floor alive with long slithering cables and crackling with sound engineers. Everywhere you went they would kind of pop up like gophers saying things like 'Five four three two testing — mind that cable, mate, it's live'.

Meanwhile, the bars had arrived in flat-packed form and a team of carpenters were puzzling over the plans and trying to fit bits marked by coloured dots together, an operation that wasn't helped by the circulating spots of the disco lights.

TeaBag was working like a maniac, hauling trolleys loaded with booze through to the bars, unstacking tables and chairs and directing a team of cleaners who were trying to locate the floor between, through and around everyone else.

Under cover of all the activity, I had managed to find an extant bar tap and had siphoned myself off a nice big glass of Coke and, as an afterthought, added a dash of Bacardi from a bottle that some guy had helpfully just screwed up on the wall. Then I'd crawled under a table with it to get some peace. I was just starting to feel the rosy glow of the Bacardi taking effect, when I heard a female voice enquiring plaintively whether anyone had seen me.

I peeped out from under the tablecloth. Franz and Justine had turned up to *lend a hand*.

I sat very still – but as luck would have it a lost sound engineer came crawling my way with a pencil behind his ear and a circuit plan between his teeth.

'There's a bloke under here,' he announced.

'Hi!' said Franz lifting a corner of the tablecloth. 'Is this a private party or can anyone join in?'

'Well . . . er.'

Without waiting for an invitation, she slid her body under the table and shifted it over very close to mine – the hussy!

'I'll get you a drink . . .' I said hurriedly and stumbled out, slopping Bacardi and Coke over her.

I was saved by Justine who was looking for a male to bang some nails into the wall.

I never did find out how long Franz waited under the table but she didn't look wildly pleased when I next saw her.

Actually, as the evening progressed, things got pretty fraught. The sound engineers had managed to get their system to the volume testing stage and we were being blasted by intermittent bursts of eardrum-bursting 'Rave'.

The carpenters finished the bar in record time and lined us all up to admire the end product.

'Looks a bit empty. Something's missing,' said Justine.

'All it needs is the barman,' said Jason.

TeaBag looked at Jason and Jason looked at TeaBag.

'We have booked a barman?'

After that Jason nearly went bananas. Eventually we all calmed him down by promising to find someone before the end of the day.

It's incredible how hard it was to find the kind of person that fitted Jason's job-description. Which basically boiled down to working virtually all night for practically nothing. I mean, I wouldn't wish a job like that on anyone.

'The guy we need has to be able to pull the girls, charm

the guys and generally spread charisma all round,' I said to Alex on the phone.

'Well, I'm not sure,' said Alex, in an offhand manner. He was still pretty huffy with me about the plaster cast episode. 'How much did you say the basic was?'

I mumbled a figure but went on to point out what a bomb he was going to make on tips; not to mention the contacts.

I could tell he was tempted, he just needed his vanity massaged a little harder.

'I mean quite frankly it's a cinch, just lounging round the bar to draw the trade, chatting up the occasional chick and mixing a real mean cocktail.'

'Well, I guess I could sleep it off during the day since I'm off school at present,' he said.

I wondered, with just a tinge of guilt, whether Alex was going to be able to cope, serving drinks with a leg in plaster. Still, to hell with it, he had both hands free, hadn't he?

By the time I had sorted Alex, Jason had started a new panic.

We could all hear him through the office door grilling TeaBag.

'But we can't open without bouncers.'

'Yo, no worries. Baby-Jo, I gave him this number, said he'd call.'

'But he hasn't, has he?'

At that point Justine hauled me off to help with the decor. This mainly consisted of her standing around with her head on one side being 'creative' and me heaving things round like a navvy doing all the work.

We found the ideal place for the Queen's portrait: overlooking the stairs so that she could vet everyone who came in. And after a lot of argument and carrying it around, we positioned the glass case, with the iguana in it, in the one warm corner near the central heating boiler, and it turned out not to be stuffed actually, just extremely slow-moving.

After that I tore down, and carted away, acres of musty velvet, and Justine said she thought the whole place looked rather bare. So I suggested that we should think of something tasteful to do with the pink naked ladies.

'How about screwing them to the wall?' said Franz handing me a screwdriver.

It seemed that this was another 'man's job'. So with a lot of tricky hole-boring and screw-driving, aided by Franz who stood by and passed the screws, placing them 'seductively' one by one between my lips like lighted cigarettes, we eventually had the ladies pinned up in a row like the victims from some medieval witch hunt.

Then Justine found a pot of gold paint and two brushes and said in a rather meaningful way to Franz that it was *her turn with the ladder.*

She handed me a brush and the two of us set about gilding the naked ladies in respectability.

'Guess who's going to be the barman,' I said as we stood back to admire our handiwork.

'Who?' asked Justine.

'Alex.'

'Oh really?' She didn't sound wildly interested. She was evidently wising up to Mr Mega-stud. Maybe this was a good moment to enlighten her about our dialogue of the other night.

'He dropped by at Chuck's the night before last,' I said. 'We had quite a revealing chat as a matter of fact.'

'What about?'

'Well, you featured pretty prominently, actually.'

'I did?'

'He implied that the two of you were pretty close at one time.'

'He did? Tell me more.'

(Hang on a minute . . . she was taking this very coolly . . . what was she up to? I'd expected her to be simply livid!)

'Well, were you? Or weren't you?' I prompted.

'Wouldn't you like to know . . .'

'Well, yes, I would actually.'

'Oh really . . . I don't think it concerns you actually,' she said.

'But it does!' I insisted.

'Oh, does it?' she said, pausing with her paintbrush poised. There was an oddly triumphant glint in her eye. 'Why?'

'I'm *interested*, that's all.'

'Are you now?' Her eyes met mine.

Oh my god . . . Geesus . . . she thought I was chatting her up.

'Yes. And I ought to be going actually.'

'So should I, term starts tomorrow. I'll be expected to get some sleep – such a drag. How about seeing me home?'

'Couldn't you take a taxi?' I asked.

Franz, on a return trip for the ladder, caught the tail-end of this.

'Chauvinist pig,' she muttered.

So naturally, under the weight of all this female blackmail, I felt obliged to see Justine back to Cheyne Walk.

We took the tube to Sloane Square, then we had to walk the rest of the way. Justine somehow managed to inveigle me into going the long way round – taking the Thames side of the Embankment – the quiet side where practically no one goes, ever.

At intervals, benches, set out invitingly in the dark patches between the lamp-posts, threatened our progress. I kept walking as fast as I could.

'Wait,' she said and leaned on the Embankment wall. I paused dutifully.

'This bit of the river always reminds me of Paris,' she said in a voice ominously charged with emotion.

'Umm . . . it is a bit niffy,' I said.

She swung round to face me.

'Have you ever noticed,' she went on. 'I mean, isn't it really odd, how people who look like each other, kind of . . . *get on*?'

Now this was a tricky one. People had obviously been noticing, and no doubt had been commenting on, our odd kind of resemblance.

'How do you mean?'

'Well, isn't it funny how *couples* so often, in a weird kind of way, look alike.'

'You mean like people tend to get to look like their dogs?'

'Well . . . yes . . . sort of . . .' said Justine, frowning at this obvious put-down.

We were both silent for a moment.

'But it is odd, isn't it?' she persisted. 'Really freaky how *we* . . . I mean, you like all the same things as me. I mean, I've never met anyone who was quite so . . . on the same wavelength before . . . like you and me . . .'

She looked me straight in the eyes. It was a look which was intense and searching. She was moving closer . . .

Oh my God . . .

Oh my God. Oh my God. Oh my God. Chuck was right. She really did have the hots for me. Typical! And this was a bad case! Like ser-i-ous, man! What was I going to *do*?

'I think . . .' I said; it came out as a sort of squeak. 'We ought to hurry. It's getting really late.'

She walked on reluctantly, staring out over the water which was reflecting back the strings of lights the kind of corny way rivers do. I padded miserably beside her. It was clear that I had to take immediate evasive action. I was somehow going to have to deflect this outbreak of passion.

'Talking of dogs. I saw a dead one in the Thames once,' I said.

'Really?'

'Yeah, it was all kind of bloated, with its legs sticking up in the air.'

'Gross,' she said and shivered.

'Are you cold?'

'Umm, I am a bit.' (I think maybe she was hoping I'd put my arm around her or something.)

'Better walk a bit faster then.'

I knew I was being really rotten to her. Oh why, out of all the 'blokes' in the world should she have chosen *me*. It was so unfair . . . I was starting to feel really sorry for her . . . correction . . . for *me*! . . . Poor, poor *me*! There I had been dreaming about, searching for, *agonizing* over finding that elusively perfect male and I had found it! And it was the very one I could never *have*. Geesus what a *mess*!

But . . . (I hesitated). Maybe I could have been mistaken? . . . I risked a glance at her. Her eyes met mine – they were all kind of . . . glistening.

No, I could not. GOD! What was I going to do?

I kept my hands firmly thrust down into my pockets and speeded up into an even more cracking pace to avoid any possibility of body contact.

When we reached Number 122, naturally Justine hovered on the doorstep.

'Won't you come in for a coffee?'

'Coffee?'

'Yes, you know – hot brown stuff.'

'No . . . thanks all the same. Last bus, you know.'

'That's not for ages.'

'Penultimate bus then.'

She put her key into the lock but didn't turn it.

'Well . . . I guess we'd better say good night then.'

She stood in the porch with her lips kind of poised, at-the-ready . . . I stared past her and said, 'Good Lord, look at that!' pointing vaguely into thin air.

'At what?'

'Thought it was a UFO.'

(I was behaving like a real nerd.)

'That's a plane heading for Heathrow,' said Justine. 'Good night.'

And she went indoors shutting the door, quite unnecessarily hard, behind her.

Fifteen

That whole scene with Justine suddenly made me reassess precisely what it was she was after. I mean, as a girl, I had kind of seen finding the Right Male as the key to Life, Happiness and the Meaning of the Universe.

Viewing it all from the–other–side as it were – the male side – I was starting to wonder – was it really such a big deal?

I mean, more than half the time 'going out' actually means 'staying in' – wasting entire evenings vegging out together in front of videos instead of experiencing the thrill–of–the–hunt round pubs and clubs and places, hot on the track of the talent. Then if you actually *went out*, as a couple, I mean – to parties, for instance, there'd be all that sitting around holding hands and looking like a pair of prize drips when everyone else was having a whale of a time getting off with each other.

I had suddenly realized that 'going out' was basically 'opting out' – losing out on all the man–hunting, all the boy–swopping – the sheer *bliss* of snogging–around.

But, of course, as things stood Justine obviously didn't see it that way. She'd set her heart on conquest. And the victim was me!

Luckily enough, thank God, she was in school all the following day so our paths didn't cross. It was Monday – the Club's opening night so I knew this respite couldn't last for long. Tonight she'd be back with a vengeance. She'd never miss such a God-given opportunity to flaunt herself around.

I had volunteered for the safest job I could find. My official new job title was Cloakroom Attendant. I was to be penned up in this kind of box which had a hole in the side for the coats to go through. I had a book of raffle tickets, a tin of pins and about two thousand dry cleaners' coat-hangers for ammunition.

Still, it had one redeeming feature: I wasn't totally out of touch. My box had a phone. Which was handy because we still hadn't heard from Baby-Jo – the bouncer. While the others went home to change into their very best opening-night-wear, Jason had left me with the last minute panic of finding someone, *anyone* who would bounce for us.

'Get anyone you can think of,' he said. 'Even if they're total physical weaklings. I simply don't care any more.'

I was about to ring Chuck when the line was barred by an incoming call.

'Mr Gladstone please, I must spick with Mr Gladstone.'

'Not you again. How many times have I told you? He's not here!' I slammed down the receiver and dialled frantically before he could call again.

'Hey, Chuck?'

'Hi!'

'You are coming tonight, aren't you?'

'Sorry, mate. Not my kind of scene,' he said.

'But you thought up the name and everything!'

'Sure but . . . I'll give it a miss, thanks. All those posey people.'

'The thing is we could do with some help actually.'

'Oh, yes?'

'We need a bouncer.'

'A bouncer! Give me a break. You know I'm a pacifist.'

166

'Please?'

'Strictly not on. . . . Tell you who might, though . . .'

Chuck gave me Matt's number.

'Hey Matt, it's me, Jake. You know – friend of Chuck's.'

'Oh yeah?' (That tone of voice was totally uncalled for.)

To up my cred, I launched into 'E-speak'.

'Know that gothic weirdscene, one we were trying to tag?'

'Yeah?'

'How's about bouncing it, like tonight, man!'

'What, put the boot in, break a few chairs?'

'No! . . . proper bouncing . . . standing around looking frightening.'

'Plus in it?'

'Sure!'

We started arguing about how much, but he said they'd come anyway and 'Get-it-sorted-later'.

I had to ring off at that point because the first people were arriving.

It was the crew from *Tatler* who had come early in order to do a shoot. There was a photographer with a guy carrying a pole with a light on, who ran around kind of attached to him by a lead like someone on a saline drip. There were two very bored models of the starved waif variety smoking furiously between yawns. And there was a woman with making-a-statement-about-myself looks – practically shaven hair, black-rimmed eyes and prune lipstick – who appeared to be in charge.

They started off by tracking down their hoard of champagne and opening a few bottles.

Once they'd loosened-up, 'Punk-Revisited' started draping the models in various poses and aiming a black-rimmed eye through the camera lens at them. Then she redraped them several different ways and stood back and shook her head.

'We should've brought a male,' she said.

Everyone looked depressed and passed around more champagne and fags and then someone said, 'How about him?'

Five pairs of paparazzi eyes were trained on me.

'Why not? He's not bad, actually,' P-R walked over to my pen. She jerked her head sideways, indicating that I should stand up.

I hauled myself to my feet.

'Not bad at all,' she eyed me up and down. 'Are you allowed out of there?. . . . We could make it worth your while.'

She took a wadge of folded notes from inside her jacket and wafted them under my nose.

I was out on the dance floor in no time.

Someone found the DJ's den and Madonna's voice was soon yearning out of the sound system. Taking their cue from her, the two models started to wind their bodies round mine.

The cameraman was directed to lie on the ground and take some right-up-the-crutch-darling angles.

'Sorry, sweety. We'll have to get that shirt off you. Livvie-luv, if you have to chew gum, can you try and time chews between shots?'

Before I could object, I found I was being stripped to the waist.

'Come on. Look as if you're enjoying yourself, for god-sake. Give him some champagne or something, someone.'

I was force-fed champagne and given a puff of someone else's fag.

(Enjoying myself! Quite frankly, I felt used.)

'No that's OK, I like it. Keep that bored-as-hell look. Do you think you could bite his ear, Shar? Harder. That's great! Hold it!'

They were just deciding on which knots to use to tie me up with the naked golden ladies when Jason arrived and bellowed up the stairwell that there wasn't anyone in the Cloakroom and so I was, most reluctantly, released.

Back in the Cloakroom I counted the money P-R had handed over. There were *three* £20 notes.

So, OK I felt used, but no one could say I'd made myself cheap.

Shortly after that, everyone else started to arrive. Actually, there's more to Cloakroom Attending than you'd think. Not only do you meet people, you get to know precisely who wears who,

Predictably, nobody obeyed the dress code. Apart, maybe, from a couple who I'll swear were cross-dressing and two boys who were wearing their baseball caps the right way round.

At about 11.00 pm Justine turned up with Franz. I had been waiting for this moment with some trepidation.

I just prayed she hadn't made a complete spectacle of herself. But no – she'd come in fighting form. Tonight this was *it*. She'd really made an effort. Actually she looked pretty impressive, even though I say it myself. She even looked OK when she turned around. It's true that the Harrod's dress did make her bottom look just that bit bigger than usual, but it simply didn't seem to matter. For once, she had what it takes to carry it off. In fact, as everyone said, in her new dress and her new shoes, she had never looked so simply *radiant*.

'Hi!' she said, as she passed over her coat, giving me, the cause of her radiance, the full blast of its effect. Then she added with a frown, 'What on earth are you doing in there?'

'Hi,' I said from the security of my box. 'This is my new job.'

'Hi,' said Franz. 'Want any help in there?'

'I don't believe it,' said Justine. 'Come on, Franz. Let's find

Jason . . .!' and she strode off as fast as her dress would allow her.

She came back about ten minutes later.

'He'll only let you out if I can find someone to replace you.'

I dumped some coats in a pile on the floor and said, 'It's OK really. I'm fine . . .' . . . 'Three coats and briefcase on the same ticket . . . OK?'

'Leave it to me!' she said and disappeared into a phone cubicle.

About three-quarters of an hour later, when I had just about exhausted the supply of hangers, a gross but familiar anorak was passed over.

'Hi!'

It was Chuck.

'Thought you said this wasn't your scene?'

'Justine virtually begged me to come,' he said with a grin, displaying a sudden burst of totally misplaced confidence.

He'd OD'd on aftershave again.

'See you 'round,' he said, and dropped a 5p into my tips tray.

I watched, as his best black school trousers disappeared up the stairs.

A few minutes later he was back with Justine.

'Honestly, it's only for half an hour or so, just to give Jake a break,' she said. 'I'll love you forever, promise.'

Chuck lifted the flap, climbed into my booth and said under his breath, 'I'll kill you for this.'

'This has nothing to do with me, honestly!' I said, as I obediently followed Justine.

'Depends how you look at it,' said Chuck grimly.

Justine led me up on to the first floor, where there was a little cordoned off square of red carpet, designated 'The VIP area'.

Inside the ropes people were huddled together wearing fixed photo-opportunity smiles and shouting at each other against the decibels of the music. From time to time the *Tatler* team swept by, hot in pursuit of some minor celeb and, as they were lost from sight, the smiles kind of slipped.

Having trapped me in this social game-reserve, Justine then proceeded quite blatantly to ignore me. She started flirting outrageously with every male in sight.

'Ha-llo,' I thought. I could see what was going on – it was so desperately transparent. She was trying to make me jealous.

I just had to stand there and helplessly watch her making a total exhibition of herself while Franz bawled something in my ear about some excruciatingly boring book she was reading.

Then Franz suggested a dance and we made a foray down to the dance floor. It was so packed there was barely room to move an elbow. So after a couple of numbers we gave up trying and forced our way back upstairs.

Justine had an empty glass in one hand and an empty bottle in the other, her hair was getting on the wild side and she had a desperate look in her eyes.

'I think Jake deserves a drink,' said Justine meaningfully to Franz.

'No, I'm fine honestly,' I said, praying that Franz wouldn't leave us alone together.

'But he can't just stand there with nothing to drink.'

'You get him one then,' said Franz moving closer.

'I can get my own, thanks,' I said, glad to have any excuse to make a getaway. On my escape route, I came face to face with Jason. He was loitering, trying to make sure, without looking obvious, that no one got more than their two-glass ration of the free *méthode-champagnoise* sparkling wine.

'How many people do you think there are in here,' he asked rubbing his hands.

I thought back to the coat-hangers.

'Must be a well over a thousand,' I said.

'Do you really think so?' he peered over the balcony. 'Chryst, you're right. We're only licensed for eight hundred.'

I was instructed to go and tell TeaBag, without attracting too much attention, not to let any more in till somebody left.

I forced my way down the stairs against the rising incoming tide of bodies. The dark suits and little black numbers of the early crowd had given way to the ripped jeans and leather gear of the late-and-lovely. All of London's 'social nobility' seemed to be there.

Downstairs, I fought my way on past the battleground of the bar. I couldn't actually see Alex through the forest of arms waving fivers. But he was obviously being run off his feet (or foot). People who had been aggressive enough to make it through to the front were doubling their orders and staggering out with orders for friends lodged further back in the crush. Something told me Alex wasn't going to have too much time on his hands for chat-ups.

I fought my way on, past the Cloakroom. I couldn't see Chuck. The hole in the wall was now totally filled with coats that had been rolled up and crushed in. A lurid vision of Chuck being smothered in designer streetwear rose to mind. Chuck of all people – what a way to go!

At last I sighted the doors . . . *and the doorman.*

TeaBag was lying across the reception desk drinking out of a bottle of the *Tatler* crew's Moët et Chandon.

As he saw me, he waved it.

'Yo . . . Jake . . . What a partyyyy . . . man.'

People were flowing past him without giving their names or paying or anything.

'TeaBag! Why are you letting all these people in?'

'They're friends, you see. Matt and Al and Fozzy – they said to let them in – any of their friends. They said let them in – or else. Yo man! They're so pop-u-lar! They must know half of London.'

I prised my way through the doors and peered outside. The queue stretched down the street for a quarter of a mile or so.

The newly recruited bouncers were sitting on the pavement, having a kind of impromptu party of their own, passing round the 'spliffs'. They were all totally stoned.

I could hear the distant, but approaching, sound of a police siren. Shortly after that, a number of police officers rudely forced their way in. First of all they picked on TeaBag who happened to be wearing his official 'emordnilaP' T-shirt.

'Name?'

'TeaBag.'

'Full name.'

'Terence Earl Ambrose Gladstone.'

'If you'd like to come this way.'

Deep in my champagne and sound-blasted brain something registered. Like a faint echo from a far distant country, I heard a voice say: 'Can I spick with Mr Gladstone please!' Oh my God!

I watched as TeaBag was led away and I just caught a glimpse of Matt and Al and Fozzy sitting in the back of the police van before they closed the doors.

I forced my way against the crowd back up to the balcony. A great slick of people was flowing down and making for the fire exits. An ambulance had arrived and a couple of ambulance men headed for the bar carrying a stretcher. After a minute or two a figure that looked like Alex was carried out, groaning. He'd obviously been overdoing it.

Justine, who must have been searching for me all over the Club, arrived through the gloom. 'Look, Franz has got a taxi waiting at the back. We've got to get out of here. There's going to be an infernal row.'

Justine was dragging me by the arm.

I shook my head.

'You go. I'm not coming with you.'

'Why not?'

Our eyes met.

'I've got to find Chuck. We can't just abandon him.'

'But what about you?'

'It doesn't matter what happens to me.'

(True maybe – but God, didn't it sound heroic!)

Below on the dance floor a number of policemen were taking names and addresses.

Justine gave me a peck on the cheek and squeezed my arm.

'Thanks,' she said. And she disappeared into the crowd.

A rather senior-looking policeman with a loud hailer was throwing his weight around stating the blindingly obvious: that we were breaching the fire regulations and that the whole place would have to be cleared.

I spent the very worst hour of my life trying to match people to their belongings. In the end we were left with three briefcases, an umbrella, five coats and three cashmere surwraps.

Underneath the last of these I found Chuck, fast asleep.

When the final guest had left and the police had looked under tables and things, they asked to speak to whoever was in charge.

The funny thing was, we couldn't find Jason anywhere.

So the police took our names and left, saying that they would be back in the morning.

Chuck and I collapsed on a pile of chairs. Chuck took his battered pack of Marlboro out of his pocket and offered it to me.

'Want one?'

I shook my head.

That's when Jason came down off the roof.

'Have they all gone?' he asked looking around nervously.

'Looks like it,' said Chuck.

'Right! Let's count the money then.'

There was one helluva row when Jason opened the drawer 'full' of takings.

Inside there were two £5 notes and a few £1 coins.

'Where's it all gone? We've been done over! I've been robbed! Geesus when I catch the bastard responsible for this, I'll shoot him!'

I didn't feel that this was the right moment to tell Jason how many people TeaBag had let in free, which must have been practically everyone. And it occurred to me that it hadn't really been TeaBag's fault anyway. It was the bouncers'. And the reason we hadn't had proper bouncers, but only Al and Matt and Fozzy, wasn't anyone's fault really . . . but mine . . . a fact that didn't help my general confidence when it came to asking for money.

I had been summoning up courage for quite some time to ask Jason about being paid. The way things looked I might as well give up waiting for courage, so I just asked anyway.

'Did I say anything about paying you?' asked Jason in a tired kind of voice.

'Well, I just assumed . . .'

'Justine said you wanted to help.'

'I know, but . . .'

'You got tips, didn't you?

I felt Chuck's 5p rolling round in my pocket.

'Come on,' said Chuck. 'Let's call it a day.'

Sixteen

Dawn was breaking as we arrived back in Ferndale Avenue. All was damp and grey and sodden. A blackbird perching on a satellite dish let out a lone throaty trill of bright notes, reminding us in an irrelevant kind of way that the world, nature and all that kind of stuff was still going strong, outside the harsh realities of our lives.

We went round to the back door, which was quieter to open than the front. The lawnmover was standing on the doormat. The cutting blades looked oddly buckled and there was a note attached to one of its handles: '*Next time you mend the mower – don't forget the brake cable.*'

Inside the kitchen there was another note stuck to the Aga saying '*What was your share of the ratatouille is burned to the base of the pan.*'

On the fridge, secured with a fridge magnet of a horny toad, was a note saying in running-out Biro '*Judie? Woke us at 12.30am! To say she'll be at Putney Fair tomorrow.*'

And beside the washing machine stuck in a pile of Chuck's clothes, that were crusted with velvet-mange and dotted with splats of gold paint, was a final one that said: '*When's he going?*'

'I don't think we're wildly popular,' said Chuck.

'Who the hell is Judie?' I asked.

'No idea.'

He filled two bowls with Coco Pops, poured milk on and we sat for a moment in silence, munching.

Then Chuck said, 'Maybe it's Jeanie, from school. The one with the lips?'

I stared at the note. 'No, it's definitely an upstroke. It's more like . . .'

Chuck grabbed the note: 'Geesus . . . it is. It's Julie!'

We had a kind of brief impromptu war-dance round the kitchen at that point.

I was all for going over to Putney right away, but Chuck pointed out that fairs didn't get going till late afternoon, and suggested that we should try to get a few hours' sleep in first.

'What about school?' I asked.

Chuck shrugged. 'I can soon catch up, no hassle.'

'What about Maggie?'

In the end we composed a note which we stuck in a prominent place on our bedroom door:

ATTACKED BY KILLER PRAWN BIRYANI – BOTH SURVIVED BUT OFF TAKE-AWAYS FOR LIFE. TAKING DAY OFF – DO NOT WAKE *PLEASE*

We were woken around four-ish by Maggie who came in making sympathetic noises and carrying two mugs of Peppermint Infusion. She said Justine was on the phone.

'Who does she want to speak to?'

'Jake,' said Maggie.

I shook my head violently, so Chuck took it.

'No, we're fine. How's Jason?'

'......'

'Oh dear.'

'......'

'No Jake can't talk to you at the moment.'

'......'

'Well, he's busy. . . . Packing.'

'.......?'

'He's had this telegram. He's got to go back to Mauritius.'

'......'

'Yes.'

'.......?'

'Well, almost immediately. This evening.'

'......!!!!'

'Look, Justine . . .'

'......'

'Uh huh.'

'......'

'Ummm.'

'......'

'OK, I'll tell him.'

'You bastard,' said Chuck, when he put down the phone.

'What have I done?'

'She was practically crying, if you'd like to know. That's all.'

He grabbed his towel and made for the shower.

Then, almost immediately, he came back through the door.

'I've just had a thought,' he said.

'What is it, now?'

'Well, it's just occurred to me that that Julie woman might well need the two of you there – I mean, how's she going to switch you over if there's nothing to switch you to?'

'So what do you suggest? I ring up Justine and say, "Hi, oh, by the way, how's about coming along to this fair this afternoon, so that I can get turned back into you?" '

'Maybe something a little more subtle than that. A "bloke" of your proven pulling power shouldn't have too much of a problem getting her to come along – use your ingenuity.' Chuck turned and headed off bathroomwards.

★

I lay for a few minutes staring up at the ceiling.

'Oh boy!'

Then I climbed out of bed and started to get dressed very slowly.

'Geesus.'

I reached for the phone and dialled her number.

'Hi, it's me.'

'I know,' she said.

'I was ringing to say goodbye.'

'So you're really going?'

'I have to . . .'

'I see . . .' She cleared her throat. 'When will you be coming back?'

'I don't know that I will,' I said.

'Mauritius is an awful long way away.'

'Oh, it's not that far,' I said.

'It is. I looked it up on my globe pencil sharpener,' she said. 'It's right round the other side . . .' her voice kind of broke.

I felt such a heel.

Chuck was hovering in the doorway with a towel round his waist.

'Get on with it . . .' he said under his breath.

'Look,' I said. 'There's still just enough time . . . to meet up, I mean . . . to say goodbye.'

'There is?'

'Yes, look, how's about we get together?'

'Where?'

'At Putney Fair?'

'Why Putney Fair?'

'Well, er . . . it's sort of on the way to Heathrow . . .'

'When?'

'Five-thirty, by the Big Wheel?'

'I'll be there,' she rang off, no doubt in headlong flight for the wardrobe in a frantic search for a last-ditch seduction outfit.

'Geesus', I said to Chuck. 'You realize this is really going to complicate matters . . .'

He shrugged, 'Well, you couldn't have left without saying goodbye, now could you?'

He made it to the bathroom. This time he actually had his shower.

I looked around the room. At any rate, there was no mad rush; I didn't have anything to pack. I checked through my pockets. Inside the jacket I found the *Tatler* £60. I located an envelope on Chuck's desk and slipped two of the notes into it and addressed it to the Kensington and Chelsea Hospital. Then I put the other £20 in Chuck's pocket.

After that I went downstairs to say goodbye and a massively grateful 'polite guest' thank you to Maggie and Casper.

Fortunately, Putney Fair on a wet September afternoon is not the most romantic of places. As we approached, we were met by a damp breath of wind carrying the whirr and moan of the rides, the deep reverberations of the generators and the jarring sound of appallingly amplified music.

I paused at the edge of the common, staring with seriously heightened perception into its jumbled mass of metal, like a madman's invention heaving and spinning, laced with tinsel-strings of coloured lights. The rank sweaty fairground smell of griddling hamburgers entered my nostrils.

Was this it? Was this to be my last sighting of life, love and eternity from a male point of view?

'Come on!' said Chuck. 'What are we waiting for?'

We squelched into the thick cloggy mulch of well-trodden grass and made for the Big Wheel.

Justine was standing right beside the Pay Kiosk. She was

marooned on a kind of stepping stone surrounded by a sea of mud, looking utterly forlorn.

But when she caught sight of me she cheered up quite a bit.

'Hi!' she said and turned and gave Chuck a kiss on each cheek and then kind of brushed her hair out of her eyes and looked the other way, so that I stood there, not knowing how to greet her, feeling like a right prat.

No one said anything for a moment.

I gave the crowd the once-over but no one who looked remotely like Julie was anywhere to be seen.

'How long have we got?' asked Justine.

'Hard to say,' I said.

'But you must know what time your flight leaves!'

'Oh that! Yes, ummm, eight o'clock.'

Justine was doing lightning miscalculations.

'That should give us a couple of hours then.'

'So let's take a look around,' said Chuck grabbing each of us by an arm and literally frog-marching us along.

We went right round the entire fair twice, without even sighting anyone with red hair or seeing anything remotely like a Photo Booth.

We came to a halt under something called the Freak-Out which went round and round and sideways and upside down with a total disregard for the fact that humans were basically designed to be kept '*this way up*'.

'Say Chuck, why don't you have a go on that, my treat?' said Justine. She pressed a fiver firmly into his hand and a foot hard on his.

Chuck exchanged glances with me.

I gave him a half-nod. Well, I felt it only right to give the girl a moment or two of my undivided. After all, it was *my heart* I was breaking.

Chuck took the hint and left the two of us alone together.

We wandered on in silence. I was searching the faces of

the crowd for Julie's bright red lips and lurid hair. I think Justine was most probably racking her brains for something 'memorable' to say.

I was starting to wonder if we'd come to the fair with false hopes, maybe that note had been from Jeanie after all . . .

It was Justine who broke the silence in the end.

'So, *do* you want to go on anything?'

What I really needed was a better view, from somewhere higher up.

'How about the Big Wheel?' I suggested.

There was something ominous about the enthusiasm with which Justine greeted this offer.

I realized with a sinking feeling that you couldn't choose anything with much more romantic potential than the Big Wheel – except maybe the Ghost Train.

We climbed into this ski-seat-made-for-two and with a lurch we were swung upwards and backwards. Lurch by lurch, we rose until we could see the whole fairground set out beneath us. And as each lurch took us upwards my heart sank deeper and deeper.

Justine had already placed her hand very close to mine.

'It's so sudden, you going away like this,' she said.

'I think perhaps it's the best thing for both of us,' I said.

She gave me a searching glance, then said, 'Admit it. You feel just the same way as I do, don't you? I can tell.'

'Well, yes, I guess I do in a funny kind of way.'

'It's all so grossly unfair, you having to go so suddenly, like this.'

'But it's probably for the best . . .' I repeated, inadequately.

'How can you say that! Geesus!'

The Big Wheel had started going round at full pelt. At regular intervals the fairground, the suburbs of Putney, the Thames and London were presenting themselves to us in rapid succession.

'Couldn't you put off going; I mean – for a week or two at least?'

I shook my head, 'I think that might be difficult.'

'Why?'

'It's just that I've got myself into something that I've got to get out of, that's all.'

'There's someone else, isn't there?'

'No, honestly, it's not that.'

'Then tell me the truth?'

'Really. It's all so complicated, you wouldn't believe me if I did.'

'Try me . . .' she said.

'Look . . . would you do something for me?'

'Anything.'

I took the envelope out of my inside pocket.

'Could you deliver this to the Kensington and Chelsea Hospital?'

She took the envelope. She stared at it as though it was poisoned or something.

'The loan. You got the money. How . . .?'

'Something came up. I had a bit of luck . . .'

'The Club's money, Jason's – you didn't . . .'

'Of course not!'

'That's why you're going away, isn't it?'

'No!'

'Look if you're in trouble, I don't care. I'll come with you. I'll do anything . . .'

'But you can't,' I said. 'Not where I'm going.'

'Mauritius isn't that far away. You said so yourself.' Her voice went all sort of 'husky' and her eyes suddenly had that kind of 'welling' look.

It made me feel really guilty. Of course, I could see now, Chuck had been right *from the very start*. I should have noticed how she blatantly didn't look at me the first time we met. And what an idiot she'd made of herself every time we'd seen each other after that. In fact, looking back on it, she'd been so-oo obvious. But, seeing it all from the male point of view – typically – I'd misread every move she'd made! Actually, I felt enormously sorry for *her* . . . correction, *for myself*.

'Look, you have to try and understand. I'm not what you think I am. I mean, basically, you hardly know me.'

'I know all I want to know,' she said with determination.

We were just coming up on an upswing when the wheel slowed in a great slurring arc and stopped dead. We were right at the top. It was very quiet up there. I couldn't see her face. She was silhouetted against the brightness of the lights below.

Her lips were coming perilously near mine.

'Chryst, what can I say to make you understand? I'm not Jake . . . bloody . . . Drake. I'm not even "real" for godsake!'

'Not *real*?'

'No . . . I'm only virtually real – just someone made up in your mind . . . you see. . . .'

At that point I happened to glance fortuitously down towards the ground . . . and I caught sight of. . . . it could only be . . . that flaming red hair . . . that dumpy little body . . . it was!

'Julie!' I roared. But my voice was drowned out by a sudden blast of reggae from the Pleasure Dome.

She was moving between the booths, at any moment she'd be lost from sight.

There was nothing else for it.

'Goodbye,' I said. And I swung my body over the side of the car.

Leading down, there was a kind of ladder which the Big Wheel guys use to replace the light-bulbs and things.

The crowd gasped as I located the first rung with my toe.

For a total physical coward, I think I made a pretty impressive descent. But, after all, my whole future was at stake.

Above, Justine's face looked down, very pale and getting

tinier and tinier. Below, the fairground guys had linked arms and were holding people back in case I fell. But I didn't. As I reached the ground, Chuck burst through the cordon.

'I've seen her . . . Julie . . .' I shouted, dodging people in a frantic attempt to make my way after her.

Chuck grabbed my jacket. 'I'm coming with you.'

'No . . . go back . . . Justine . . . grab her when she gets off and come after me . . .'

I shot down a narrow gap between the Ghost Train and the Candyfloss stall and caught a tiny glimpse of red hair disappearing behind a crowd of kids with Mickey Mouse balloons. She had slipped through between two shooting booths . . .

'Julie . . .' I shouted.

I raced on, heavy mud clogging my boots, weighing them down and slowing my progress. It was like running in a nightmare.

In between the booths it was dark . . . I couldn't see my way . . . I tripped on a guy rope and fell. Geesus!

As I opened my eyes I found was staring directly at a mud-encrusted scarlet stiletto heel.

'Looking for me?'

'Julie . . . thank God I've found you. Please, you've got to change me back.'

She was standing in front of this absolutely massive van that had written on its side, in very new-looking stick-on vinyl letters:

ALTERNATIVE YOU plc
COSMESTIC CONSULTATIONS. COLOUR ADVISORY. BEAUTY THERAPY.

'You'd better come inside,' she said.

I followed her up some steps. Inside the van everything was very stark and clinical and had a strong new-car-smell.

In the corner I could see a booth very much like the one in Olympia; a bit battered but patched up and resprayed.

'Now what's the problem?' she said, studying my face. 'Too much on the chin? Did we go overboard on the ears or what?'

I explained that it was a little more fundamental than that.

Her eyes widened. 'You did go to town, didn't you? When was this exactly? I'll have to find your disk.'

When I told her the time and place she said, 'Oh dear. Oh my God, I do remember you now.'

'That's good.'

'No it's not. I hardly like to tell you this but – all those disks were destroyed.'

My heart dropped a couple of kilometers.

'This explains how you got stuck like that,' she continued. 'It was only meant to be a demonstration, you know.'

'You mean you can't change me back?' I could feel my palms going icy cold and damp with panic.

'Well, it'll be tricky,' she said. 'And you're going to need your original on hand, of course.'

'It's OK, she's on her way,' I said, casting a hasty glance out through the door of the van. Chuck and Justine were nowhere to be seen.

'Well, I suppose you could make a start while we're waiting,' she said. 'Provided you can remember what you looked like before.'

She directed me into the booth and pulled the curtain across.

I sat facing my face.

I started twiddling the vertical knob. And then the horizontal. I kept trying things and changing my mind. I got my skin colour back to normal but surely my nose used to be smaller than that?

Julie was fussing about outside.

'How are you getting on?'

'Well, I still can't get the chin right, it doesn't really look much like me.'

It was at that moment that I heard a frantic banging on the door.

'He's in there, I know he is. Let me in!' It was Justine's voice.

Then I heard the van door being opened and Chuck's voice.

'Did a boy come in here, blond – about six foot two?'

And then Julie's voice: 'Come on in, we've been waiting for you. Right, I can see the likeness now. Just pop inside and take a seat. It won't take a moment.'

'What is this, what's going on? Where's Jake?' Justine's voice was half suspicious and half furious.

'Go on Justine.' Chuck's voice had an urgent note in it.

'I'm not moving until I've found Jake.'

There was no way she was going to see me like this – I was neither one thing nor the other for godsake.

There were sounds of a kind of scuffle and then Justine's face appeared looking very cross indeed, staring through the two-way mirror into mine.

As she caught sight of me – a look of total shocked disbelief crossed her face . . .

'Oh my God!' she said.

'*Quick*, press Switch,' shouted Julie.

I banged my palm flat down on the button.

The screen pixilated all over and then it cleared quite suddenly. I could still see my reflection staring back at me, just as it was before. Even my chicken-pox scar was intact. Big deal.

Outside I could hear the scream and whirr of the rides.

Tentatively I drew back the curtain.

'Everything OK?' asked a voice.

It was Julie.

'I think so . . .' I said.

'Watch how you go now.'

I staggered out of the booth. I was feeling really pretty exhausted for some reason.

I glanced at my watch. Five minutes to go before I was due to meet Chuck at the main Entrance, if I could ever find it.

I had practically retraced my steps to the Space Race Experience when a voice came over the tannoy system telling us to clear the building because there was a 'Security Alert'. A Fire Alarm began to ring.

The whole of Olympia immediately went into panic mode and started stampeding for the fire exits.

I was kind of borne along by the crowd and before I knew it I was swept out through the emergency doors into the street. I struggled along through the massed bodies as we swarmed across to the other side. Searching through the crowds, quite suddenly, I caught sight of a familiar back. It was Chuck's. Forcing my way through the people I made my way towards him.

'Chuck,' I shouted.

I grabbed him by the arm.

That's when I was hit by the most mind-blowingly vivid 'déjà vu' experience I've ever had.

And then it all came flooding back to me.

'GEESUS!'